PERILOUS MASQUERADE

Linda would do anything for her sister — she'd had her fair share of problems. But Julia's unusual request resulted in Linda having to work in Greece, posing as the mother of her nephew, Nickie. It was a perilous masquerade, but for the child's sake — and Julia's — she daren't let the mask slip. But when she found herself falling in love with Andrew Duncan, her boss, how she wished that she could reveal her true identity, and her feelings.

Books by Stella Kent
in the Linford Romance Library:

THE CAUTIOUS HEART
PROUD CITADEL
CLAUDIA ON THE WING

STELLA KENT

PERILOUS MASQUERADE

Complete and Unabridged

LINFORD
Leicester

First published in Great Britain in 1985

First Linford Edition
published 2010

British Library CIP Data

Kent, Stella, *1930 – 1977*
  Perilous masquerade. - -
  (Linford romance library)
  1. Love stories.
  2. Large type books.
  I. Title II. Series
  823.9'14–dc22

  ISBN 978–1–44480–223–8

Published by
F. A. Thorpe (Publishing)
Anstey, Leicestershire

Set by Words & Graphics Ltd.
Anstey, Leicestershire
Printed and bound in Great Britain by
T. J. International Ltd., Padstow, Cornwall

This book is printed on acid-free paper

1

'Julie, I can't! I'm sorry, but I simply can't.' Linda Blair tried not to see her sister's face. 'I'm not allowed to have people staying at the flat. Mr. Belvedere particularly said so, and I don't want to lose my job. I was lucky to get it, with a decent place to live.'

'But Linda, I've no one else to turn to! We'll be as quiet as mice. Your Mr. Belvedere will never know we're here.'

Reluctantly, Linda forced herself to look at her sister. Her eyes red from weeping, her little son clinging to her skirt, she was a sight to melt the hardest heart — and that was something Linda was far from possessing.

Playing for time, she said, 'Let's get Nickie away from the discussion. We're upsetting him.' She gathered the child into her arms. 'How about a nap, sweetheart? Linda has bought you a new picture-book. You can look at it while you have your rest.'

The little boy's dark curly head drooped into her neck as she carried him into her bedroom. 'Lindy, read me a story,' he murmured.

'Yes, darling. As soon as you've had a sleep.' Linda lowered the child on to the bed, tucked her duvet around him, and handed him the picture-book. She dropped a kiss on his forehead and stopped in the kitchen to make a pot of coffee before returning to the sitting room.

At the sight that met her eyes, her heart sank. Julie was curled up in the corner of the settee, snivelling forlornly.

Linda felt a momentary stab of resentment. Julie was less than two years her junior, yet sometimes, Linda felt that her whole life had been a sequence of rescuing her sister from one heedless mess after another.

As Linda poured the coffee, Julie gave a final sniff and broke into her train of thought. 'I know I've been an idiot before — lots of times, and you've always helped me out. But, surely you can see, this time is different.'

It was exactly what Linda had been thinking herself. This time it was different because Nickie was involved.

She passed Julie her coffee-cup. 'Tell me again what happened. Maybe you imagined it.'

Julie shivered. 'I wish I had! But, no. For two mornings, a car has been parked a little way along the street from Nickie's nursery school. Two Italians were sitting in it watching the children come out. Waiting — ' her voice trembled — 'waiting to snatch Nickie.'

'Paolo *was* allowed access,' Linda murmured.

'He would keep him, I know he would. He'd take him back to Italy and all those horrible Mancinis. I'd never see him again.'

Linda reflected briefly that only three years ago, the Mancini family — wealthy, handsome, sophisticated — had represented all that was most desirable to Julie.

'How do you know they were Italian?' she asked flatly.

'I can always tell. If Sister Mary Joseph hadn't let us out the back door, Nickie would be far away by now.'

'Keep him at home for the time being.'

'That's just playing for time. They only have to ask one of the other mothers where I live.'

* * *

Linda pondered while she drank her coffee. She had felt some sympathy for Paolo Mancini during the fearsome marital squabbles and even more violent divorce proceedings. He was spoilt, headstrong and immature, but never vicious until he fell under the influence of his dissolute elder brother, Bernardo. In fact, his ebullient charm had a certain appeal, and he undoubtedly loved his wife and son in his fashion. Nevertheless, she believed that

4

Julie's fear of Nickie being snatched had a real foundation.

'Why do you get involved with these ghastly macho types?' she asked sourly. 'There was that Spaniard — Carlos, or whatever his name was. And that lifeguard at Rimini. How can you stand their arrogance? Why can't you take up with someone who respects you as a person?'

'Like David?' Julie put in slyly.

'Not necessarily — ' Linda caught herself up crossly. 'And why not like David? He's kind and thoughtful — '

'And a monumental bore!'

'He's not a bore. He's a very pleasant companion.'

'You're right,' Julie soothed. 'Only — he's not exactly exciting, is he?'

'Where has excitement got you, except being reduced to a sodden wreck at regular intervals? But this is irrelevant.' Linda didn't want to discuss her long-term, and undeniably lukewarm, relationship with David Halliday with her sister. Their mutual dislike was too long-established and probably quite irreversible.

'About staying here,' Julie said, sensing Linda's defences were down. 'It would only be for a short time. I've got a job and accommodation lined up in Bristol. It's just not available for a while.'

'How long?'

'A month at most. We won't be any trouble. I'll take Nico out during the day.'

'Nickie,' Linda corrected automatically. These throwbacks to Julie's enthusiasm for all things Latin irritated her. 'It wouldn't be fair to him. He's only three. We can't expect him to be quiet all the time.'

'You said old Belvedere doesn't spend much time here, now that you know the ropes.'

'He does spend more time at salerooms, now,' Linda conceded. She had been flattered that, after only two months, Adrian Belvedere trusted her to manage his high-class antique shop full of exquisite and valuable things.

She had been lucky to get the job. While Julie was off on her Italian adventure, married to the youngest son of the Mancini hotel empire, she had been nursing her father through his last illness. When he died, the family home had been sold to pay off debts and medical bills, and she was left with neither home nor job. Exhausted and upset, her secretarial skills rusty, she had not felt ready for the competitive pressurised business world.

The job at the antique shop and the pleasant flat above it, provided a respite while she regained her confidence. True, her salary was small and Adrian Belvedere was not an easy boss, but the work was fascinating and she had learned a lot.

Julie watched hopefully as misgivings clouded Linda's grey eyes. 'Please, say we can come,' she whispered.

Linda was lost. Julie was once again the little girl crying on her first day at school over the broken doll.

'All right,' she agreed reluctantly. 'But you'll have to move out as soon as you find somewhere else — or if Mr. Belvedere turns nasty. I simply must keep this job.'

'Oh, Linda, thank you!' Julie leapt from the settee and hugged her sister warmly. 'I'll leave here as soon as it's dark, pack everything up and get a taxi back.' She beamed at Linda. 'I knew I could rely on you to know what to do. You're so — so experienced.'

'No,' Linda thought bitterly. 'What I am is responsible. I trained for a career and worked at it. I nursed our father. You travelled the world, you had lovers, and married, and had a child — it's you who had the experience.' But there was no point in saying it aloud. She didn't even know if she would have taken advantage of freedom from responsibility if she had had it. She was no risk-taker and she knew it.

★ ★ ★

She cleared away the coffee things and washed them, then emptied a drawer and made space in the wardrobe, helped by Julie, who was chattering happily now that she'd got her own way.

Watching Linda carry the duvet and spare pillows through to the settee, she observed, 'David is going to be pretty mad at us taking over the bed.'

Linda looked up. 'It's nothing to do with him.'

Julie grinned wickedly. 'I thought not, somehow!'

Irritated, Linda set about getting a meal. She had no intention of telling Julie that the bedroom played no part in her relationship with David, that, in fact, he had only set foot in the flat on two brief occasions.

When her father had been ill, entertaining friends at home had been difficult. She had seen David a couple of times a month for a film, or a meal, and been glad of his company. Now that she was alone, there was no reason why he shouldn't visit her at the flat but, somehow, she hadn't got round to suggesting it, and David hadn't pressed for an invitation with any great ardour.

She put her reflections to one side and concentrated on more pressing problems. They finished their meal, Nickie was put to bed and, as darkness fell on the early May evening, Julie stole out of the flat with a great deal of theatrical furtiveness.

Linda picked up Nickie's picture-book and together they selected a story. Against all the odds, he was a well-behaved, lovable child, unaffected by the outrageous spoiling he had received from both his parents and, in the three weeks since Julie had returned to England, Linda had become very fond of him, baby-sitting him two or three times a week when Julie revital-ised her social life.

Julie arrived back at ten o'clock with as much drama as she had departed, and the girls unpacked and stowed away her belongings — Julie in high spirits, Linda not without misgivings as she recalled her employer's sour intolerant face. Somehow she didn't think that Adrian Belvedere was a child lover.

But for a few days all went well. Mr. Belvedere only spent a couple of hours each day at the shop. Nickie behaved angelically. The days were mild and Julie, as she had promised, spent a lot of time outdoors with him.

At the end of the week, Linda invited David to supper with the idea of reconciling him and Julie. It was not a complete success. Her two guests behaved courteously to each other but, when she went downstairs to see David off, he turned in the hallway and exploded in exasperation.

'So Julie's taking advantage of you once again. Don't you think it's time she stood on her own feet? She's twenty-two years old. Are you going to go on mothering her for ever?'

Linda hastily pulled the inner door shut. 'I don't know what you mean, David.'

'She's hiding out here, isn't she?'

'It's only for a short while. She has a place lined up in a couple of weeks.'

'Why is she here? Why has she left her own flat? If she's hiding from Mancini, you're both in a pretty dubious position legally. He was granted access to his son.'

He looked down at her from his long, lean height. He was pleasant-looking, rather than good-looking. His thick reddish-brown hair was brushed neatly back and his steady grey eyes were solemn. The fact that he seemed older than his years stemmed more from manner than actual appearance.

'We know that, David,' Linda said appeasingly. 'But Paolo is totally unreasonable at the moment. I believe he's quite capable of snatching Nickie. When they've both cooled down a bit and can behave more rationally — ' Her voice tailed off. People behaving irrationally was something David couldn't possibly understand.

He fidgeted with his car-keys, his

expression slightly sheepish. 'Look, Linda. You do understand I can't risk getting involved in this? I'm sorry, but my career is far from being established — '

Linda felt a little chill. 'I realise that, David. I had no intention of involving you.'

Their goodnight was brief and cool before David turned away hurriedly to his car.

★   ★   ★

She went back upstairs where Julie's face told her that she could guess at their conversation.

'David doesn't approve of this, does he?' she asked.

Linda shrugged slightly. 'You know David. He's a bit — cautious.'

'I'll say he is! You'd think he was ninety! What you need, my girl, is someone madly impetuous and un-predictable. Mix the two of you up together and you'd both come out about right!'

Linda didn't answer. There was probably something in what Julie said but, in practice, the attraction of opposites didn't seem all that common. Being the sort of person she was, she was attracted to safe and predictable men like David, and they seemed to react in the same way.

In the bathroom, as she prepared for bed, she let down her immaculate knot of hair. She peered in the mirror at it hanging in soft, sensuous golden waves around her white shoulders. Maybe if someone was to see her like this? But, of course, they never did. Keeping her guard up had become a way of life to her. She slipped into her boyish cotton pyjamas, tied her hair back with a piece of ribbon and made for the settee.

The following day Adrian Belvedere left for a two-day porcelain sale in Edinburgh and the girls were able to relax. It had turned cool and Julie was glad to stay indoors. The sisters romped with Nickie until the middle of Monday afternoon, when Mr. Belvedere suddenly arrived at the shop in a filthy temper, having been outbid for every lot he had coveted.

He flounced around the shop, his voice querulous, his well-manicured hands fluttering.

'My dear, £1,200 for quite second-class Chelsea! It was absurd and, in my opinion, something distinctly shady was going on. And a perfectly foul hotel — the sheets quite grey!'

Linda plied him with coffee, relieved that Julie had taken Nickie to the playground. But, as she assumed a sympathetic expression, she listened anxiously for their footsteps in the hall. It was a chilly day and Julie couldn't be expected to stay out for very long.

But just at that moment, Adrian Belvedere was distracted by the discreet ping of the bell above the door. Two men had entered and were looking around them. Both were young and dark, their suits were expensive, and there was a good deal of gold at their hands and wrists. To the shopkeeper they looked like promising customers and, smiling, he advanced to meet them. To Linda, with a suddenly lurching heart, they looked only Italian.

Coarsely handsome and menacing, they seemed to fill the little shop.

'Good afternoon, gentlemen,' Mr. Belvedere enunciated hopefully. 'Can I help you? Or do you just want a little browse?'

The larger of the two men looked at Mr. Belvedere as though he was some strange bug.

'We look for a woman,' he said in an unmistakably Italian accent. Linda's heart flopped completely and she began to sidle towards the door at the back of the shop.

'A woman!' Adrian Belvedere's high-pitched voice rose to a squeak. 'My dear sir, what kind of an establishment do you think this is?'

The intruder elbowed him aside and both men muscled their way further into the shop.

16

'We hear you keep woman here,' Number One insisted.

'I assure you, I do not,' Belvedere squealed. 'That is my assistant, Miss Blair. She's the only woman on the premises and I can't imagine she would have any business with you!'

The first Italian stared at Linda, the thick black curls over his low brow enhancing his bull-like appearance.

'You Julie Mancini?' he demanded hoarsely of her. 'You hide little Nico here?'

Linda cleared her throat and miraculously found her voice. 'No,' she croaked. 'My name is Linda Blair.'

The man stared at her, then at Adrian Belvedere, and finally at his partner. Reasoning of any complexity obviously did not come easy to him.

At last he said threateningly, 'If you lie, we come back — and you don't like!'

★   ★   ★

17

The two men strode from the shop and Mr. Belvedere sank into a chair. He pulled out a silk handkerchief and mopped his brow. 'What perfectly frightful people! Whatever can he have meant? Of course, there is a very undesirable element moving into the neighbourhood — I presume you don't know anything about it, Miss Blair?'

Linda's thoughts raced round like squirrels in a cage. Should she confess everything to her employer and throw them all on his discretion? He seemed an unlikely champion but, with the likelihood of further unpleasant developments, was it fair to keep him in the dark?

The decision was taken out of her hands. At just that moment, Nickie, who had never previously shown the slightest interest in the shop, flung open the door that connected it to the hallway with a crash that set the delicate china and glass on display tinkling perilously. He took one look at Adrian Belvedere, who had left his chair and appeared to be advancing on Linda, and opened his mouth wide.

'Mama,' he wailed. 'Nasty man in Lindy's shop!'

In the seconds that Belvedere took to recover his senses, Linda bundled Nickie out of the shop to join Julie, who was standing horror-struck behind him. As she heard their footsteps scurrying up the stairs, she turned to face her employer, now scarlet-faced and spluttering apoplectically. As she looked at him, all thoughts of throwing themselves on his mercy fled.

And she was right. A brief, but honest, résumé of the circumstances brought forth such a vicious attack on her integrity that she found her cheeks flaming and her own voice rising in defence.

But Belvedere was not to be moved. After a hysterical demand that all three of them leave the premises immediately — 'before your Mafia friends return!' — he finally conceded that Linda was entitled to a week's notice.

Somehow, the last hour of business dragged past until, at five o'clock, Linda was free to escape upstairs to the flat.

She found Julie waiting for her, contrite and subdued.

'I'm sorry, Linda. Nickie just opened the door before I could stop him. Did you manage to talk Mr. Belvedere round?'

'No, I'm afraid not. But it's worse than that.' Linda sank on to the settee. 'Paolo has traced you here. He sent a couple of thugs to the shop this afternoon. They had just finished putting the fear of God into Mr. Belvedere when Nickie popped in. They must have missed you by seconds. Anyway, the end result is we've all got our marching orders.'

Julie's face whitened. 'Who were they? Not Bernardo?'

Julie was convinced — and Linda thought correctly — that Paolo's dissolute older brother had contributed largely to the break-up of her marriage.

His resentment at seeing his former companion in debauchery settling into a happy stable relationship had been obvious from the beginning.

'No, not Bernardo.' Linda shuddered. She had vivid memories of Bernardo's single-minded pursuit of her at Julie's wedding. 'I didn't recognise them, but they're probably relatives of yours. I think I convinced them for the time being, but don't delude yourself. If they come back again, Mr. B. will lose no time in telling all.'

Julie digested this. 'And you've got the sack? Oh, Linda, I'm so sorry. Do you think if I talked to Mr. Belvedere — told him that Nickie and I would leave right away — he would keep you on?'

'No, I'm sure he wouldn't. It's me he's mad at. In any case, where would you and Nickie go?'

'When do we have to leave?'

'We have a week.'

* * *

Big tears began to form in Julie's wide blue eyes, then brimmed over on to her cheeks. 'I'm sorry. I've messed things up for you again.'

'There's no point in going into that now.' Nickie was looking distressed as he watched his mother, and Linda summoned a bright smile. She poured him a mug of milk and fetched a biscuit from the tin. 'Don't worry. We'll think of something.'

'But what?' Julie snivelled hopelessly. 'Where can we go? We'll have to move quickly. Paolo's men could come back at any time.'

The thought had not been far from Linda's mind. She could not imagine that Paolo would wish to hurt them, but the men had been alarmingly aggressive and might well get carried away in the execution of their mission.

A hotel was out of the question. They had very little money between them and Linda's small salarly was only sufficient to cover essentials. What was more, during Julie's three years

22

abroad and Linda's two spent nursing her father, any friends who would have given them shelter seemed to have married and disappeared from the scene.

Suddenly, Julie, who had made a brief effort to rally her spirits for Nickie's sake, shuddered convulsively.

'I forgot to tell you. Something happened while we were out this afternoon. That's what I had on my mind as we came in. That's why I wasn't watching Nickie.'

Linda looked at her fearfully. 'Do you think the men saw you?'

'No, it wasn't anything to do with them. It was while we were still in the park. I happened to run into Liz Daley. Do you remember her? We worked together for a while just before I was married. Well, she's at Heathrow, now. She works in the booking hall. And she told me that Paolo had been hanging around for days. Either Paolo, or one of his brothers — every day. She thought maybe I was arriving and they weren't sure of the flight.'

'Did she speak to them?'

'No.'

'What did you tell her?'

'The truth. That we were divorced now and I didn't want anything more to do with him, and I asked her not to tell them she had seen me. I know she won't but, Linda, you see what this means?'

'Yes,' Linda said bleakly. 'If they are watching Heathrow, they'll be watching other airports — and seaports, too. And there are enough tentacles to the Mancini family to cover every outlet in Britain.'

The sisters lapsed into a helpless silence. They prepared a meal for Nickie and themselves, but their own was largely left uneaten. Afterwards, they cleared up and put Nickie to bed. From time to time, one of them would start to suggest some possible course of action, only for her voice to falter and die away.

As soon as it grew dark, Linda slipped down to the corner newsagent and bought copies of all the unsold papers. Returning to the flat, she divided the *Situations Vacant* pages between them and silence reigned for a while as they studied them silently.

It was a disheartening operation. It wouldn't have been difficult for Linda to find a job. Even for the largely unskilled and untrained Julie, something might have been found. But living accommodation wasn't available with anything for which she was qualified, and there was certainly no place for Nickie.

After about ten minutes, Julie said wistfully, 'Listen to this, Lin. '*Live-in receptionist wanted for exclusive health and beauty clinic in the Home Counties.*' That would be great for me. I really enjoy working as a receptionist and I've got a diploma in beauty therapy.'

'But what about Nickie?'

'Well, of course, they wouldn't have Nickie. I meant, if I didn't have him.'

'Well, you have, haven't you? So it's hardly helpful,' Linda snapped.

*   *   *

They continued in silence for another ten minutes, the only sound being the rustle of paper as one section after another was exhausted and joined the growing pile on the floor. Then, just audibly, Linda read, *"Child not objected to'.'*

Julie looked up hopefully. 'What is it?'

Linda read the advertisement through to herself, then she shook her head regretfully. 'No — sorry. That's no good.'

'What do they want?'

"Secretary/assistant required by business man for a short period. Must be prepared to leave Britain immediately. Child not objected to', Linda read aloud.

'But, Linda, that's perfect!'

'Except that you're not qualified for secretarial work.'

'I've worked in offices. I can file and do two-finger typing.'

26

'I think employers' expectations are usually pitched a little higher than that. What about shorthand?'

'I can write quickly.'

'It's not the same thing.' Linda read the advertisement again slowly. 'There's something rather odd about it,' she said.

'What do you mean?'

'Applicants have to contact a Mrs. MacIntyre at the Alistair Duncan Shipping Company. That couldn't be more respectable. The Alistair Duncan Company is a big, old-established business. But doesn't it strike you as a bit desperate? *'Prepared to leave Britain immediately. Child not objected to.'* That's a strange provision for a secretary. It's as though they hadn't been able to get anyone.'

'So you think it's worth a try?'

'Anything's worth a try,' Linda said firmly. 'We've certainly got nothing to lose.'

''*Leave Britain immediately*',' Julie mused. 'For where, I wonder?'

'Probably some God-forsaken white-man's grave,' Linda replied. 'That might account for them not being able to fill it.'

They continued their search through the remaining newspapers, but nothing else remotely possible came to light. As the sisters retired to sleep, they were resolved to contact their only hope, the reassuring-sounding Mrs. MacIntyre, at the first opportunity.

★ ★ ★

It was, of course, Linda who made the call.

'You'll create a better impression,' Julie pleaded. 'You know how flustered I get. You sound so calm and competent. What does it matter? Our voices are similar.'

So, with the misgiving that had haunted her since Julie's arrival at the flat, Linda picked up the receiver.

The girls were in the little cubby hole, behind a large desk in the corner of the shop, that Adrian Belvedere used as an office. Linda dialled the number given in the advertisement and, in a few moments, was connected with Mrs. MacIntyre. The woman's friendly voice, with its soft Highland lilt, was immediately reassuring.

'The job would entail accompanying Mr. Andrew Duncan to Greece for a period of three months at most,' she explained. 'To act as his secretary for three or four hours daily.'

'And that's all?' Linda queried. She was unable to keep the suspicion out of her voice. 'I mean, it sounds such a highly desirable position. May I ask why you have made allowance for applicants with a child?'

'No, it isn't quite all,' the woman confided. 'And that's where we're having the difficulty. The provision for a child is not an inducement, but a positive advantage. The position is this. Sir Alistair Duncan's little granddaughter, Katina, lives permanently in Greece and is becoming quite Hellenicised. It distressed him very much, the last time he visited, to find that she could scarcely speak, or understand, English. So, the other part of your duties would be to talk with the little girl and help her with her English. And another English child to play with would, in my opinion, bring her on faster than anything.'

'I see,' Linda said slowly. The clouds that had weighed so heavily on her began to drift away. This job, if only she could secure it for her, seemed the perfect tailor-made answer to Julie's problems.

'How old is the little girl?' she asked.

'She's five years old. The daughter of Sir Alistair's older son. You may remember he was tragically killed in a plane crash last year. What age is your own child — Ms?' she appended tactfully.

'Ms Blair,' Linda said. 'He's only three years old, but he speaks very well.'

'And you are an experienced office worker? Well, that sounds ideal. You wouldn't believe the difficulty we've been having, although we're prepared to offer an excellent salary,' she enlarged chattily. 'First-rate secretaries who run a mile when you mention a child, and perfect ninnies who wouldn't know a word-processor if it bit them. So, you'd be interested in coming in for an interview, Ms Blair? And a few tests?'

The euphoria that had lapped Linda for the past few minutes suddenly ebbed away.

'Tests?' she echoed faintly.

'Of your speeds. Oh, I'm sure you'll do splendidly. Under the circumstances, Mr. Duncan won't expect the perfect secretary but, at the same time, he does like his work done neatly and efficiently.'

Linda looked at Julie, the fluffy curls tumbling over her forehead, the wide blue eyes still hopeful against all the odds. The living, breathing prototype of Mrs. MacIntyre's perfect ninny. Then the sharp slam of a car door arrested her attention, and she looked out to see Adrian Belvedere advancing across the pavement towards the shop like an infuriated turkey-cock. She couldn't bring herself to crush their only hope.

'Yes. Yes, I would be interested,' she babbled into the phone. 'When could I come, Mrs. MacIntyre?'

She had just replaced the receiver when Adrian Belvedere charged into the shop. 'Making ourselves quite at home, are we?' he squeaked. 'Don't let me interrupt your calls.'

'It was just one local call,' Linda said shortly. She put her hand in her skirt pocket and found some silver that she laid on the desk. A warm flush coloured her cheeks. 'I have to try to find alternative accommodation for my sister and myself. As I can't leave the shop unattended, this is the only means open to me.'

'Since when has the well-being of my shop concerned you?' Belvedere sneered. 'Oh, get off upstairs and lay your plans there. If your charming friends return, it's better that you're out of sight.'

Julie put her small, soft hand on his sleeve and turned on him the appealing eyes that had melted a score of obdurate hearts.

'I'm awfully sorry, Mr. Belvedere,' she whispered. 'It's completely my fault.'

Adrian Belvedere jerked his arm away as though a tarantula had come to rest on it. 'I'm perfectly aware of that,' he replied icily.

'Come on, Julie, it's no use,' Linda said. She took Julie's arm and steered her back upstairs to the flat where Nickie, still in his pyjamas, was playing contentedly.

★ ★ ★

Julie started to get his breakfast. 'What exactly did the woman say?' she asked Linda. 'I couldn't make it all out. You looked hopeful at one point. Then the temperature seemed to drop when you said 'tests'.'

'Of your speeds — shorthand and typing.'

'Oh,' Julie said hollowly. She put Nickie's egg on the table and cut his toast into 'soldiers'. 'Then it's no good, is it?'

'No. I'm sorry if I raised your hopes. It was just that, up until then, it had sounded like the answer to our prayers.'

'But still, you made an appointment. You're going to see them?'

Linda looked at her sister blankly. '*You're* going to see them. I was speaking on your behalf, remember?'

'Oh, of course. I forgot. But — you gave them your name. Miss Blair.'

'The chief qualification for the job at that stage seemed to be speaking decent English and having an English-speaking child. Nickie looks Italian anyway, to saddle him with a name like Mancini would have been a stroke against him, quite apart from the possibility of that clan getting wind of what we're up to.'

'But there's no point in me going, Linda. Honestly, my typing is rotten, and I can't do shorthand at all.'

'I suppose not.' Linda was still reluctant to abandon their only hope. 'The interview isn't until ten o'clock tomorrow,' she went on. 'There's a typewriter in the shop. After Mr. Belvedere leaves, we could spend the whole evening working up your speed. Maybe you could get by.'

'Linda, that's just ridiculous! I'm a slow learner. I couldn't pick up touch-typing in a month, let alone one evening.'

Linda knew that Julie was right. 'Then we'll write it off. Don't worry, something else will turn up.' She tossed the paper on top of the others that they had exhausted.

'No,' Julie said. 'Don't do that.' She retrieved the newspaper from the pile. 'There's only one answer. You must take the job.'

Linda looked at her, puzzled. 'That's no solution. The problem is over *your* job. I can get one without much difficulty. And I certainly don't want to go abroad and leave you and Nickie to Paolo's tender mercies.'

'No,' Julie said again. 'You don't understand. I meant that you could take Nickie with you. As his mother.'

Linda stared at her. 'You're not serious?' she said at last.

'I'm perfectly serious. You'll get the job easily. It would get Nickie safely out of the country. They're watching the airports, remember. They'd certainly spot me, but they probably wouldn't notice Nickie with you. Not many of the Mancinis know you.'

Linda was still staring. Not only at the sheer outrageousness of the suggestion, but in amazement that her helpless, muddle-headed sister should have come up with such an audacious plan.

'No,' she said at last, faintly. 'It would never work. Nickie wouldn't go with me.'

'Go with Lindy,' Nickie chirped happily, stretching out his arms towards her.

The gesture spurred Julie to greater efforts.

'Of course he would,' she asserted. 'He adores you.'

'But — he wouldn't remember to call me Mummy.'

'There's no need. A lot of children call their parents by their first names. And, if he should make some slip, he'll be surrounded by Greek people who wouldn't notice it. I don't suppose this Mr. Duncan will be very concerned about your relationship to Nickie anyway, as long as you do your job all right.'

Linda was still impressed at how persuasively Julie could argue a case when it advanced her own interests. 'No,' she said again. 'I can't do it. Your own claim to Nickie is tenuous enough — my having charge of him would be quite illegal.'

'It's only until Paolo cools down and finds some other interest. Oh, can't you be a little adventurous for once!'

'It isn't that,' Linda said, although

she knew there was truth in Julie's accusation. 'It's deceit — and you know I hate that. Forget it, Julie, we'll just have to find something else.'

Julie knew from past experience that when Linda had made up her mind she wasn't to be shaken and, a little sulkily, she dropped the subject.

After lunch Linda collected the day's papers and, once again, they repeated their search of the previous evening, but there was nothing new. Only the Duncan advertisement still shone, like a beacon, out of the reams of newsprint.

Linda was still adamant. 'We'll go to the Employment Office first thing in the morning,' she determined. 'Maybe they will have something.'

2

When she awoke the next morning, it was to find Julie standing over the settee, pale and shaking.

'Julie!' Linda snatched at the slipping duvet. 'Whatever's the matter?'

'Look out of the window!' Julie whispered.

Cautiously, Linda approached the window above the street and tweaked back the curtain. On the opposite side of the road, a large black car was parked. Inside, Linda could make out the two men who had visited the shop.

Julie, her brief lacy nightie contrasting with Linda's cotton pyjamas, clutched at her arm. 'Are those the men?' she breathed. 'The ones who came to the shop?'

Linda nodded, her face as pale as Julie's.

'How can we get out of the house?'

Julie wailed. 'We can't get to the Employment Office, or anywhere else.'

Desperately, Linda pulled her thoughts together. 'There's a bus,' she said. 'It stops outside the shop, every ten minutes. If we rush out and jump on — '

'Not with Nickie,' Julie said firmly. 'I'm not going to let them see him. I don't think they're sure we're here, or they would have barged their way in. I think they're hoping you'll lead them to me.'

'Then maybe I can lead them away from here.' Linda began to pull on her clothes with fingers clumsy with panic. 'Will you be all right here?'

'I hope so.' Julie nodded. 'Oh, Linda, I'm sorry I've brought this on you.'

'It's too late for that, now.' Linda impatiently brushed her honey-coloured mane of hair and swirled it up into a pleat at the back of her head. 'I'll be back as soon as the coast is clear.'

'Here's the bus, now,' Julie called urgently.

Linda watched with her as it

lumbered round the corner, then, timing her flight, she dashed down the stairs and out of the street door, just as the bus drew in to the stop.

She waited with feverish impatience as a passenger alighted, while making sure that the two men in the car noticed her departure. As the bus drew away, she was relieved to see the car start up in pursuit.

She rode four stages until the bus turned a corner and stopped at a busy intersection. Linda leapt off and darted into a department store. Safely inside the entrance, she watched as the big black limousine cruised past.

She heaved a sigh of relief. She noticed a coffee-shop advertised on an upper floor and went up on the escalator. In her headlong flight from the flat, there had been no time for breakfast. She collected a strong cup of coffee and sat down.

The coffee did little to steady her as she endeavoured to organise her thoughts. Julie and Nickie must be moved, that was the first essential. If only she had felt able to ask David to take them into his roomy apartment. But instinct told her that he would not take kindly to the suggestion, otherwise he would surely have made it himself.

She could go to the Employment Office — it was only five minutes walk away. And ask for what? A job with accommodation to begin immediately? For a girl with Julie's meagre qualifications, plus a child, it wasn't very hopeful in a time of such high unemployment.

★ ★ ★

She glanced at the clock. It was nine forty-five. She was also only five minutes walk from the Duncan Shipping Company office. And there lay a job that answered perfectly their requirements, if only Julie possessed the qualifications. Linda heard again Mrs. MacIntyre's warm, comfortable voice, reminding her slightly of her own mother's. It had been the voice of sanctuary.

Almost automatically, she found herself getting to her feet. What had she got to lose by going to the interview? If she didn't get the job, no harm was done. If she was offered it — but she refused to let her mind dwell on that possibility.

She slipped into the cloakroom and regarded her reflection in the mirror. She noted her pallor, but not her undeniable beauty that, far from stress-ing, some stubborn instinct in her understated. She didn't see the fine bone structure, the wide grey eyes and softly curved mouth, or the thick, dark-honey coloured hair. She only saw that she was not dressed as she would have chosen to go to a job interview. She gave a shrug, picked up her bag and left the cloakroom.

Outside the store, she kept to the inside of the pavement, keeping an anxious watch on the passing traffic, but she saw no sign of the black car and, in a few minutes, she had reached the huge, opulent, brick-and-glass building that was the headquarters of the Duncan shipping line.

In the big marble foyer, she paused to get her bearings, scanning the notice-boards that listed departments. She noted a heading, 'Katrakis-Duncan, Athens', and guessed that this could be the destination of the successful applicant. Then she spotted 'Isobel MacIntyre, Personnel', with a room number on the second floor, and headed for the stairs.

The room turned out to be an outer office, where a young woman inter-rupted her typing to take Linda's name into the inner office. In a moment she returned, motioning Linda to go in.

Mrs. MacIntyre, seated behind her desk in the pleasant, sunny office, was exactly as Linda had imagined her. Fiftyish, a little plump, with sympa-thetic eyes behind spectacles, and a warm smile.

'Ah, come in, Ms Blair,' she said, as

Linda peeped shyly round the door. 'I don't mind telling you — although I shouldn't — that my hopes are riding on you. You wouldn't believe the types we've had in here. All after an expenses-paid holiday in Greece, with nothing to offer on their part at all.'

'I don't have anything like that in mind.' Linda smiled.

'I can see you don't. You're quite a different type. Sit down, my dear. Fiona will bring us some coffee and we'll have a little talk.'

The girl was summoned from the outer office and Linda relaxed and expanded under Mrs. MacIntyre's gentle questioning. She told of her experience in other jobs and offered references. Then Mrs. MacIntyre gave her a few simple tests that she passed with flying colours.

'You're exactly what we wanted!' the older woman exclaimed in delight. 'I'll tell you, now, you as good as got the job over the telephone yesterday. You demonstrated the essential requirement.'

Linda looked at her in smiling mystification.

'Your delightful speaking voice,' Mrs. MacIntyre expanded. 'Are you Scottish?'

'Yes, although I came south when I was very young.'

'You still have a slight intonation. Sir Alistair will be delighted. He's so anxious for his granddaughter to speak good English — and for him that means with a slight Scottish accent! You won't actually be expected to look after her, of course. She has a nursemaid, and there are other servants, but they are all Greek, so such English as Katina speaks is very accented. Apart from that, you will only be required to do a little secretarial work for Mr. Andrew.'

* * *

Belatedly, Linda realised that the job would almost have been within Julie's capabilities — and that would have solved their problems in a much more straightforward way. But there was no way she could introduce a substitute at this stage. It looked as though she was drifting towards going through with Julie's bizarre plan. Her heart beat wildly, but Mrs. MacIntyre's reassuring voice, coupled with the fact that she had shown little curiosity about Linda's personal life, calmed her somewhat.

Mrs. MacIntyre was outlining the practical arrangements. The generous salary, the company plane that would leave a private airfield in a little over forty-eight hours, the company car that would collect her. An advance on her salary was tactfully offered and Linda accepted gratefully.

When all the details had been finalised, Linda left the building, her mind in a whirl, and still by no means sure that she could carry off the masquerade, that Nickie would go with her, or that Julie really was prepared to part with him for so long.

She reached the shop to find Julie waiting for her, white with tension.

'Oh, Linda,' she exploded, the moment she opened the door. 'Thank goodness, you're all right. I've been so worried. Those men followed your bus.'

'I know — I managed to give them the slip. Have they been back here?'

'Not yet. I've kept watch at the window.'

'Well, for heaven's sake, don't let them see you.' Linda sat down and drew a steadying breath. 'Julie, I've been quite mad, I don't know what came over me — '

Julie sat down opposite her. 'You went to that interview,' she hazarded, 'and you took the job.'

Linda nodded shakily. 'I've got it if I want it.'

'Didn't you accept it?'

'I suppose I did. Oh, Julie, I must have been crazy. I can't go through with it — I simply can't!'

'Why not? Was there something wrong with it?'

'No, it was perfect. Well within my capabilities, a good salary, leaving by private plane from a private airfield in forty-eight hours.'

'So, what's the problem?'

'Oh, Julie, can't you see? It's you that should be going! This way — I'd be living a lie. So many things could go wrong. Nickie would get homesick for you — '

'I don't think he would. He's very fond of you. Oh, Linda, please do this for me, there's so much at stake! You needn't stay three months, as soon as I've found somewhere safe, you can pack it in.'

There was a long pause. Linda dared not look at Julie gazing so desperately at her. After a minute she said weakly, 'But what about you? What will you do?'

'Don't worry about me. I shall apply for that job at the health farm.'

As far as Julie was concerned, it was settled. With great misgivings, Linda packed her meagre summer wardrobe, augmented by two gorgeous dinner dresses and some deliciously frothy items of nightwear that she could see no possible use for, pressed on her by Julie.

Julie was in high spirits. There had been no further appearance of the Mancinis' men, and she had landed the health farm job over the telephone. To Linda's irritation, she had begun to treat the whole situation as an exciting adventure.

'What will you be?' she asked. 'Widow, divorced, unwed mum? You'll have to show your passport, you know. You can't just waltz through Customs, even on tycoons' private planes.'

'I'm aware of that,' Linda responded shortly. 'I suppose I'd better be divorced and revert to my maiden name. What about Nicky?'

'That's no problem. He can be added to your passport. We'll go to the Passport Office first thing tomorrow. It's going to be a fantastic lark!' Julie giggled. 'I'm beginning to wish I was going.'

'Believe me, so do I,' Linda said fervently. It was no adventure to her, but a precarious deception fraught with embarrassment.

* * *

One problem was what, if anything, to tell David. He had never shown much interest in her plans but, on the other hand, she had never dropped out of sight completely for three months. The dilemma was solved by him phoning on her last evening to invite her to dinner the following night.

Linda told him that she wasn't available and, when he went on to suggest other times, she was reluctantly forced to tell him that she was leaving the country at noon the following day. David was obviously disturbed by her unusual caginess and it was clear that he suspected Julie's involvement. But he seemed genuinely upset at her departure and, when he finally rang off, Linda was left feeling depressed at the fracture of her only romance, unsatisfactory as it had been.

Julie attempted to inject a party atmosphere into their last night, but Linda could feel nothing but apprehension. She woke the following morning with a headache. She derived a little pleasure from taking her leave of Adrian Belvedere before her notice had run out. Then Julie departed for her train to her new job, having taken a lengthy and emotional farewell of Nickie that reduced him to tears.

Linda was furious. For two days they had worked up an eager anticipation in him at the prospect of a holiday with 'Lindy' and now it was all undone. But, by the time the car arrived at noon, she had restored him to something like his usual happy frame of mind.

As the uniformed, obviously Greek, chauffeur carried their luggage out to the car, Linda quickly checked her appearance in the mirror. She was a little pale, with a look of strain about her eyes and a hint of smudgy shadows beneath them, but her smooth coronet of hair, and the blue cotton dress topped by a crisp, white linen jacket, looked reassuringly efficient.

Nickie, in new brown shorts and a yellow shirt, was looking up at her apprehensively.

Linda bent and gave him a hug.

'Isn't this exciting, Nickie? We're going to have such fun.'

Nickie clung to her tightly. 'Where's Mummy gone?' he whispered.

'I told you, sweetheart. She has to go to a boring old job for a little while. You wouldn't like it at all. You're coming with Lindy and we'll have a lovely time.'

He still looked a little doubtful, but managed a shaky smile. Taking his hand, Linda picked up her hand-luggage and descended the stairs.

The driver opened the car door for them and soon they were threading their way through the city traffic towards the outskirts of London. Linda passed a couple of remarks to the driver, but he seemed to know little English and she concentrated on pointing out things of interest to an excited Nickie who knelt on the seat, his face pressed against the window.

In less than thirty minutes they had reached the airfield where half-a-dozen planes of varying size were either at rest or taxiing about. They drew into a car-park and the silent driver nodded at a big maroon Mercedes.

'Mr. Duncan's car.' Then he drove across the tarmac to a blue and white plane somewhat larger than Linda had expected. 'That Mr. Duncan's plane.'

He got Linda's suitcase out of the boot and the three of them started across the tarmac. Well and truly distracted by the planes, Nickie skipped along asking a stream of questions.

They had almost reached the glass-fronted departure-lounge when, to Linda's horror, she heard a savage squeal of tyres behind her, followed by the slam of a car door. She dared not look round, but quickened her foot-steps, dragging Nickie by the hand. To be caught by the Mancinis just fifty yards from safety was too cruel a blow.

$\star$ $\star$ $\star$

Then a voice called, 'Linda!' She spun round, relief mingling with amazement, to see David.

'David! What on earth are you doing here?'

'I followed you. You were so cagey yesterday on the phone, I knew something was going on.'

The Greek driver had stopped and was looking from one to the other of them.

'It's — just a friend come to say goodbye,' Linda told him. 'I won't be a moment.'

The man strode on with the luggage and Linda followed more slowly with David and Nickie.

'This is some hare-brained scheme of Julie's, isn't it?' David demanded.

'No, it isn't. I'm leaving on a temporary job.'

'But, you're taking Nickie with you!'

'I have to. Julie simply couldn't find anything where she could have him.'

Through the polished glass window of the departure-lounge, Linda could see a small group of people regarding them with interest.

They had stopped in front of the building and David took her by the arms, pulling her round to face him.

'Linda,' he said earnestly. 'Please think again, even now. You have your own life to live, Julie is using you again.'

Linda looked up into his worried face. 'I'm sorry, David. There was just no alternative.'

'Why didn't you ask for my help?'

'You didn't want to get involved, remember?' Immediately she took pity on his shamefaced expression. 'And I didn't want you involved. It's better that you aren't. It's only for a short time.'

'But — what about us?'

Linda looked at him wryly. 'I wasn't aware that there was any *us*.'

'That's ridiculous! Surely you know how I feel about you? I wasn't in a position to say anything yet — '

Linda became aware of a stir of impatience from the waiting passengers. She tried to pull her arms away. 'I'm sorry, David, I really am. I'll be in touch with you.'

He looked down at her for a moment, then, to her horrified embarrassment, crushed her to him and kissed her with a fervour that he had never before demonstrated.

Linda pulled away from him and pushed through the heavy plate-glass doors with Nickie. She put up a hand to secure an uncharacteristically unruly tendril of hair that had escaped during the encounter and looked across the room at the little knot of people who stood waiting for her.

They were four in number, the chauffeur, Mrs. MacIntyre, and two other men.

One of the men, plump and fiftyish, was smiling at her understandingly. It was from the other man that ripples of impatience were emanating. In his early thirties, tall and markedly handsome, with a deep tan, thick dark hair and almost black eyes beneath winging brows, everything about him exemplified the arrogant Latin male.

'One there for Julie,' Linda thought wryly.

She advanced towards the older man. 'Mr. Duncan?' she said. 'I'm Linda Blair.'

'No, my dear.' The man took her offered hand and shook it warmly. 'I'm John Cameron, chief accountant.' He indicated the younger man. 'This is Andrew Duncan.'

★ ★ ★

With a sinking feeling of dismay, Linda turned to the second man, who was now regarding her with barely concealed antipathy. Here was not the safe haven that his name and the personality of Mrs. MacIntyre had suggested, but an overbearing male of exactly the type she most disliked and distrusted. However, her and Nickie's fate lay in his hands, and she summoned a smile to convey the cool competence that David's dramatic appearance had done much to undermine.

'I hope I haven't delayed you, Mr. Duncan,' she said, extending her hand again.

The man took her hand for the briefest possible contact. 'We are ready for departure.' His deep resonant voice held the very slight suggestion of a foreign accent. 'If you're finished with your goodbyes.' He nodded towards the window where David could be seen gazing in like a small boy outside a candy-store.

Linda sketched an irritated, dismissive wave at him.

Mrs. MacIntyre handed over some papers in a briefcase to Andrew Duncan, said a warm goodbye to Linda and Nickie and took her departure with the accountant. Then Duncan, the chauffeur bearing her luggage, and Linda, hurrying behind the men's long-legged stride, Nickie in tow, made their way through Customs and the passport check and across the tarmac to the company plane.

A handsome young Greek in a smart livery ran down the plane steps and took Linda's case from the chauffeur, eyeing her appreciatively as he did so.

Nickie was clamouring in great excitement. 'We going in plane, Lindy?'

'Yes, darling.' Linda had picked him up in her arms to ascend the steep steps of the plane when, rather to her surprise, Duncan took him from her, motioning her to go ahead unencumbered.

Inside the plane she was faced with a comfortable, though functional, lounge, with half-a-dozen seats, and tables arranged to give working surfaces. Through half-drawn curtains to the rear, she glimpsed a small kitchen.

Duncan deposited Nickie on a seat and took off his jacket to reveal a dazzling white shirt that set off his deep tan. He adjusted Nickie's seat belt, then turned to stoop over Linda.

Realising his intentions, Linda's hands flew to fasten her own belt, only to meet Andrew Duncan's hands, warm and strong, already at her waist. His eyes, less than twelve inches away, met hers, and she thought there was a hint of mocking laughter in their depths.

'Don't be alarmed, Miss Blair,' he said. 'I'm merely making sure that you're secure.'

Linda could feel the warmth of his body and smell the subtle fragrance of his aftershave. At his sudden proximity, her breath seemed paralysed in her throat and the overwhelming effect of what she had always regarded as mere animal magnetism irritated and alarmed her.

With the back of his hand beneath the shoulder-strap, he guided it from her shoulder to her waist, then sat down opposite her and adjusted his own belt.

'What is the boy's name?' he asked.

'Nickie.' Linda cleared her throat, but couldn't think of another word to say.

'Have you had lunch?'

'No.' The morning had been so crowded with action and emotion that eating had been the last thing on her mind.

'Dion will fix us something shortly.' He glanced out of the window. 'We're airborne now, can you manage the belts?'

Linda assured him quickly that she could, and he unfastened his own and turned his attention from her, taking some papers from his briefcase and spreading them over a table.

★ ★ ★

After about half-an-hour, just as Nickie was beginning to get a little restive, Andrew Duncan gave a shout; Dion appeared and Duncan spoke to him in Greek.

'I told him we'd have lunch, now, if that's all right with you?' he said to Linda.

'Yes. Thank you,' Linda said, praying that Nickie's usually good table-manners wouldn't desert him in his excitement.

Dion returned from the kitchen area with drinks on a tray, then began to set one of the tables for lunch. He still eyed her in the speculative way of the Mediterranean male that she so much disliked, suggestive of a confident belief that he was God's gift to the sex-starved Northern female. And it made it worse that Duncan was quite aware of his employee's blatant appreciation.

The steward set the table with a light meal of chicken and salad, accompanied by a white wine, and Duncan took his place opposite Linda at the tiny table. In the enclosed space, his powerful magnetism once more had the effect of making her heart race uncomfortably in her throat, and she busied herself tucking Nickie's napkin around his neck.

As she slid a cushion under him to raise him to the table, Andrew Duncan remarked, 'I'm sorry we don't come supplied with high chairs. I wasn't prepared for a young child.'

'No, I imagine you were hoping for

one a little older.'

'I wasn't *hoping* for one at all. In fact, as Mrs. MacIntyre only informed me of her unconventional appointment five minutes before you arrived, you can understand that I was somewhat taken aback.'

Linda looked at him in dismay. 'Unconventional appointment?'

'To hire someone with a child.'

'Then it wasn't your idea?'

'Definitely not. It was something cooked up between Mrs. MacIntyre and my father, who is supposed to be retired from this firm, but finds the fact difficult to remember.'

'As far as I could gather, Sir Alistair was thinking more of his granddaughter than the firm on this occasion,' Linda ventured.

'I dare say. But all I required was an efficient English-speaking secretary.'

Linda flushed. 'I assure you, you will find me that,' she said shortly. 'I'm sorry we have come as such an unpleasant surprise to you, but I have no objection to giving the little girl some instruction, and I certainly won't allow Nickie to be a nuisance.'

'That's just the point, Miss Blair.' Duncan's dark eyes regarded her coolly. 'I don't *want* my niece instructed in the ways of Western women. I don't particularly want her to speak English. This is an old bone of contention in the family that needn't concern you but, as far as I am concerned, I would prefer Katina to grow up as the daughter of a Greek house.'

And that meant a male-dominated house where a girl made no decisions for herself but simply did as her menfolk bid her, Linda thought, but she said only, 'You're employing me, Mr. Duncan. I'll take whatever line you prefer with Katina.'

* * *

She wondered why a man with a name like Andrew Duncan, son and heir of an old Scottish firm, should be so insistent on stressing the Greek half of his heritage — for he must surely have a Greek mother.

Nickie had been eating tidily and with appreciation, but now he paused and gave Andrew Duncan his full attention.

'Daddy?' he essayed hopefully.

Linda's cheeks flamed scarlet. 'No, Nickie, of course it's not Daddy.' She cleaned Nickie's hands and mouth on his napkin, aware of Duncan's sardonic gaze directed at her.

Although taller and older, Andrew Duncan did bear a superficial resemblance to the Mancini brothers with his darkly handsome looks, but his arrogance seemed to stem from character and intellect rather than the petted wilfulness of spoiled boys.

She helped Nickie to finish his meal and Dion cleared away their plates, returning in a minute with a delicious-looking dessert. He grinned engagingly at Nickie who smiled shyly back.

'Daddy?' he tried again. Then, 'Uncle?'

'The boy doesn't seem too sure of his relationships,' Duncan murmured.

'He — he hasn't seen his father for some time,' Linda explained. 'And I suppose our — going away with you confuses him.'

'And, no doubt, he has many 'uncles',' he observed smoothly.

His meaning was obvious but, although Linda's eyes flashed with anger, she decided to ignore it. 'As a matter-of-fact, he has,' she said.

'Including the precipitate young man at the airfield?'

'David? No.'

'Indeed? He certainly gave the impression that he had some claim on you.'

Linda raised her chin. 'No one has a claim on me, Mr. Duncan.'

'Ah — an emancipated woman! I'm afraid I don't have much experience of them. In Greece the woman is content to be the man's responsibility.'

'So I believe. I *do* have some experience of the Latin male.'

'A Greek is Hellenic, not Latin. You imply your experience was not agreeable. You could not perhaps have your own way?'

'It was not first-hand experience, I'm happy to say. But I have observed it.'

Andrew Duncan refilled her wine glass. 'Well, I hope you don't find it too dull with us, Miss Blair. The Villa Minerva is very quiet for a lot of the time.'

'That sounds fine to me,' Linda said sincerely. 'I prefer a quiet life.'

'That I can promise you. I am alone there most of the time with Katina. I live rather a hectic life, dashing about the world, and when I have the chance to return to Greece for a few weeks, I like to be perfectly peaceful.'

'It must be rather lonely for the little girl.'

'Yes, it is,' he admitted. 'Maybe it wasn't such a bad idea of Mrs. Mac's to import some young company. But we are visited a couple of times a month by my young cousins from Athens and then things are livelier.'

So far he had not mentioned a wife. It was no concern of hers, of course, whether or not he was married, but it was surely natural to wonder.

She said, 'Is the villa near the sea?'

'Yes, it's right on the sea. 25 km from Athens.'

'Seaside?' Nickie interjected hopefully. He turned a honey-smeared face towards them.

Duncan gave him his full attention. 'Yes, seaside. And we also have a swimming-pool. Do you swim, young man?'

'Swim?' Nickie echoed doubtfully. 'I like seaside.'

Andrew Duncan smiled and his stern face softened. 'Then you should be happy with us.' He turned to Linda. 'Would he like a nap? There's a bunk behind that curtain that I use on long flights.'

'That might be a good idea,' Linda said, surprised by his thoughtfulness. 'He had an early start and a lot of excitement.'

Nickie protested half-heartedly, but was won over by the concealed bunk, where he allowed himself to be tucked under a rug.

* * *

When she returned, Andrew Duncan was pouring coffee for them. 'After this, I must put in another hour of work,' he apologised, nodding at the paper-strewn table. 'By the way, what do I call you? Miss Blair — or is it Ms? — sounds a little formal in our circumstances.'

'Call me Linda. If that isn't too unbusinesslike.'

'Not at all. In Britain I'm known as Mr. Andrew, which sounds ridiculously feudal. In Greece I am simply Andreas.'

He pronounced the name with a proud ring and Linda smiled ruefully to herself. It would seem that her Scot considered himself a fully-fledged Greek.

She sipped her coffee. 'Don't you

find it a little confusing?' she queried.

'In some ways the races are not dissimilar — in any case, I'm stuck with it. My father married a Greek girl and found himself inextricably tied in with her father's shipping company. After her father died, her two brothers took over.'

'The Katrakis?' Linda murmured and, at his look of enquiry, added, 'I noticed the name in the foyer of your office building.'

'That's right. My uncles, Dimitri and Theo. But to return to my father. He unfortunately discovered, fairly early on, that he didn't like Greece. There was nothing personal about it. He only wholeheartedly approves of Scotland and quite a small area of that! So he concentrated on the UK side of the business and left Greece to the Greeks. I was only twelve when my mother died and, as my father had to be away on business a lot, I was sent to Athens to be brought up with my uncle's children, surrounded by Greek

71

aunts and uncles and cousins.'

He smiled. 'You'd be surprised how strong an influence Greek aunts can be, whereas I only saw Scotland for perhaps one month in a year. That accounts for my curious dichotomy.' He sobered. 'But now Robert, my brother, is dead, and my father has retired to his Scottish glen, I'm rarely able to spend long in either place. Now, if you'll excuse me, I must get on with some work. Finish the coffee, and there are some magazines behind your seat.'

He returned to the table where his papers were spread out and was soon wholly involved in them. Linda decided against reading matter and further coffee and, resting her head on the back of the seat, she studied her new employer from beneath lowered lids.

She could sense a driving dynamism in his lean and powerful body, and his arrogantly modelled face, with its long mouth and almost hawk-like nose, was filled with energy and impatience. He was nobody's fool, Linda thought with a shiver of apprehension, and she didn't care to dwell on the consequences for anybody who tried to make him one.

But, on the whole, after a prickly start, things seemed to be going incredibly well. Nickie was behaving beautifully and seemed quite happy to be with her. Andrew Duncan appeared to be a courteous and thoughtful man. It was true he had a somewhat extreme dislike of over-emancipated women, but Linda was confident she could play down her more overt symptoms. It was unsettling that he was so devastatingly attractive, but fortunate, she told herself firmly, that it was in that spectacular Mediterranean fashion that had little appeal for her.

So far, so good, she thought, stifling a yawn as her thick lashes drooped more heavily on to her cheeks.

3

She woke to find Andrew Duncan gently shaking her shoulder. 'We'll be touching down in a few minutes. Better get your things together.'

Linda looked eagerly out of the window. A little ahead of them she could see the clustered buildings of the city spreading out into greyish-green countryside, patchworked here and there with splashes of a deeper, lusher green. Against this background, a score of ancient monuments were etched. Startlingly white columns and temples, some hugely dramatic, some as delicate as filigree. And, all around the coastline, the brilliant blue sea crawled, dotted by a rash of tiny islands.

Andrew Duncan was leaning over her, also looking out of the window, his muscular body so close to hers that, once again, despite her enchantment with the panorama below, she was intensely conscious of his nearness.

'It's beautiful,' she murmured breathlessly. She turned awkwardly in the confined space and he stood back to allow her to slide out of her seat. She washed and tidied her hair, then woke and washed Nickie. They strapped themselves in for landing and, in a few minutes, were alighting on the tarmac of Athens airport.

Duncan spoke for a few moments with the aircrew and shook their hands. Then, with Linda and Nickie, he was quickly ushered through Customs and, carrying Linda's case, led them to where his car was waiting.

It was very warm, the sky was a deep cloudless blue and the sun seemed to creep right into Linda's bones. Duncan stowed her case in the back of the car and threw his jacket on top. He loosened his shirt at the neck to reveal his deeply-tanned throat. As the sun touched them, a metamorphosis seemed to come over him. The slightly inhibited formality had gone and there was a sensual, almost animal, grace about his movements. As he got into the car, he turned to smile at her — a slow lazy smile that turned her bones to water — and she prayed that the old gods of Greece would not work their ancient magic on her.

She took Nickie on her lap to look out of the window. He was still a little sleepy and cross, and she fervently hoped he wouldn't want his mother as bedtime approached. Andrew Duncan spoke little as he negotiated the chaotic traffic of the disappointingly unattractive industrial suburb but, as they began to clear the city, he said, 'You can look now.'

Linda, who had been looking avidly since they left the airport, turned to him questioningly.

'I mean, the early stages are pretty grim. Most of the city is entirely modern and rather characterless, and the suburbs are creeping farther out every month. There are even a few hotels going up near the villa but, so far, we've managed to retain our privacy.'

'Have your family owned the villa long, Mr. Duncan?'

He grimaced. 'It's Andreas, now. Weren't you aware of the transition?'

She had been all too aware of the transition, though whether she could bring herself to address him, or even think of him, as Andreas was another matter.

'My father bought the villa when I was born,' he was explaining. 'Thirty-two years ago. It was for my mother to take the family out of Athens during the summer — my brother was two years old at that time. My mother loved the villa very much — she planned the gardens. I spent a great deal of my childhood there after she died, with my aunts and younger cousins. My brother shared my father's prejudices and, as soon as he was old enough, took off for Scotland to fish and shoot in all manner of filthy weather!'

* * *

Although the city had now fallen behind them, the country still had a tamed suburban look of neat villas framed in small formal gardens, but they turned into a secondary road and gradually these fell away. They were replaced by a greenish-grey plain enclosed by low hills, smudgy with sheets of paler grey asphodel and riven with small streams and rocky paths along which grew wild fig trees and twisted aloes. Andreas turned into what was little more than a track and after some minutes in which they had not passed a single dwelling, he said, 'Look ahead!'

Linda looked straight ahead to a haze of blue where the sea met the horizon. The road wound on for a little further until they came to an extensive plantation of trees standing out dark and glossy against the dusty grey of the *maquis*. Through the trees, she caught glimpses of an expanse of sea so glittering that it almost hurt the eyes. Between the trees and the sea could be seen the long, low outline of the Villa Minerva.

They reached the top of a rise and it was possible to see where the sea met the shore in a series of little coves and inlets each carpeted with a fringe of pale golden sand. Half-a-dozen islands could be discerned far out in the bay, hazy in the heat, looking like slumbering beasts that had just reared up to bask under the sun.

Linda gazed at the scene, enchanted. Then the car descended the rise, skirted the cedar grove and came to a halt in front of the villa.

It was built of pale honey-coloured marble, not enormous, but perfectly proportioned. The porch over the front door was carried on in a portico along the whole front of the house, affording the front rooms some protection from the sun's glare, and was continued beyond the house on both sides in the form of a wall of arches, separated by

79

slender pillars clustered with vine. In the centre of the lawn they had circled, a plane tree gave welcome shade and, at the edge of the lawn, a riot of colourful shrubs bloomed.

As she gazed about her, a man and woman came through the arch of the portico adjoining the house and hastened towards the car. Both looked to be in their early forties, very dark and squarely built. They greeted Andreas warmly in Greek, glancing with shy curiosity at Linda and Nickie. Andreas got out and handed Linda's suitcase to the man.

'This is Tomas, and his wife, Eleni,' he said to Linda. 'They look after me. This is Kyria Blair.'

He didn't explain her presence any further, but opened the car door for her to get out.

Eleni held out her arms eagerly, greeting the waking Nickie with soothing little cries, 'Ah, *mikros ena*!'

Linda gladly handed Nickie over. She stood up, stretching her cramped limbs and attempted to straighten the front of her dress where Nickie's warm body had creased it. Andreas stretched, too, with the indolent grace and strength of an animal. Then they stood regarding each other warily, intensely aware of the intimate domestic tableau they must make in this unlooked-for situation.

Then Andreas said, 'Welcome to Villa Minerva.' They turned to follow Tomas and Eleni into the house.

They entered a big, square hall that was delightfully cool. It was marble-floored, apart from a few jewel-coloured rugs. There was little furniture, just a couple of heavy leather chairs, and studded antique leather chests. A number of doors opened off the hall to right and left and, straight ahead of them, was a broad marble staircase.

Andreas turned to her. 'Eleni will show you your room. She had not prepared for a child, but I'm sure she won't be at a loss. I dine at eight but, if you want any refreshment before that, just let Eleni know.'

* ★ ★

He turned on his heel and disappeared through a door on his right, and Linda followed Tomas and Eleni up the stairs. Directly at the top of the staircase, the manservant opened a door and Linda found herself in a large, beautifully furnished bedroom. Tomas put down her suitcase and withdrew. Nickie wriggled indignantly out of Eleni's arms and flew to the window.

Not knowing how much the servant knew of the situation, Linda said, 'You know I've come to work for Mr. Duncan for a short time?'

'Mr. Andreas say he bring woman back,' Eleni responded. 'He don't say about baby.'

'No, he didn't know about Nickie. I hope — I mean, I don't want to put you to any inconvenience.'

Eleni seemed only to speak the most basic English and that with a very strong accent, but she understood Linda's figure-of-speech.

'Is no trouble. Very nice baby. Katina will like him. See, next to your room is room with little bed.'

She opened a door off the bedroom to display what had probably once been a dressing room, but was now furnished with a small bed and pretty nursery furniture. 'Long ago, the madames Katrakis like to hear their babies in the night.'

'Oh, that's perfect! Thank you, Eleni.' As the woman turned to leave, Linda added, 'Is Katina about? Shall I meet her tonight?'

'She is in her bath. Soon she will come to greet you. Will the little one come to the kitchen to eat supper? Then Espasia will bath him and put him to bed.'

Linda turned to Nickie doubtfully. He had already had a lot of new experiences, and met a lot of strangers, for one day.

'Will you go with this lady and have some supper, Nickie? You'll meet the little girl who lives here. I'll see you again very soon, and you're going to sleep in this room right next to mine.'

Nickie looked a trifle apprehensively at Eleni, then back to Linda. 'Lindy won't go away?'

'Of course I won't go away. I'm going to take a bath while you have your supper.' She kissed him firmly. 'Off you go!'

Reassured, Nickie skipped across and took Eleni's hand, and Linda thanked heaven that he was such an easy-going child.

Left alone, she slipped off her shoes and approached the window. The view was heavenly. The room was at the front of the house, almost above the porch, and beyond the branches of the giant plane tree she could see a wide expanse of sea, almost violet now in the encroaching dusk. A faint intoxicating smell of lemon, lavender and jasmine, mixed with aromatic scents that she couldn't identify, rose on the evening air like stored sunshine.

She didn't know how long she stayed

there, gazing out, before she finally tore herself away. In the luxuriously appointed bathroom that was revealed behind another door in her room, she shed her travel-weary clothes and had a long, refreshing soak.

* * *

Slipping on her sensible dressing-gown in preference to the frivolous scrap Julie had insisted on packing, Linda towelled her hair dry. She then unpacked Nickie's and her own things, and put them away, their meagre belongings almost lost in the lavish storage space.

After long consideration, she selected a rose-coloured jersey dress, with clinging lines that flattered her figure, to wear at dinner with her employer. She hesitated for a moment over whether to leave her hair loose and flowing, before winding it up into its usual restrained style. It wasn't a date, for heaven's sake, she thought. And, although Andreas Duncan had self-control enough to mask his reactions, she had caught a look of appreciation in his eyes more than once and she wanted no complications of that sort. She applied a little light make-up, and had just fastened a slim gold chain around her neck when she heard footsteps and children's laughing voices approaching her door.

Relieved that the children's initial encounter seemed to have gone well, she hastened to open the door. Nickie stood in the doorway, a plumply-pretty young Greek woman behind him and, in the rear, a small girl, her eyes shining with pleasure at the unexpected arrival of a playmate.

Nickie shouted, 'Mummy, this is Katina. She lives here. She's nearly six!'

The 'Mummy' had slipped out in excitement. At any other time, Linda would have corrected him, but now she welcomed the mistake.

'Hush, Nickie!' She laughed. She smiled at the little girl. She had been expecting a Greek child, but Katina's hair, done in old-fashioned ringlets, was only mid-brown and her eyes were blue-grey. She remembered that the child's father had been only half-Greek and her mother possibly not Greek at all.

'Hello, Katina,' she said.

Katina emerged from behind her nurse and Linda saw that she wore an elaborate embroidered and beribboned white dress that, in England, would only have been worn at the most formal party.

'*Kalispéra thespinis*,' the child whispered shyly.

Linda looked at the young servant girl. 'And you're . . . ?'

'Espasia,' the girl supplied. 'I bath Nickie, no?'

'Well — if he'll let you,' Linda said. She looked at Nickie who had run across to the broad window-sill where he knelt looking out.

'It *is* the seaside,' he shouted. 'Eleni says tomorrow we can go to the beach and paddle.'

'That will be lovely. But, right now, it's long past your bedtime. Espasia is going to bath you and put you to bed. I'm going downstairs to have my supper, but I promise to come up and say good night before you go to sleep. All right?'

'Or'right,' he replied, his nose still pressed against the window.

'Is all right — you go,' Espasia said confidently to Linda and, with a last glance at the rapt Nickie, Linda slipped out of the room.

★   ★   ★

She walked down the wide staircase trying to control the shaking of her legs. The arrival of the children had distracted her for a few minutes but, now, such agitation washed over her that her usual competent self would not have recognised this creature with the dry throat and trembling hands.

She paused in the hall looking at the closed doors around her, and wishing herself a thousand miles away. Then Eleni appeared from the back of the hall and, with a smile, opened a door to her right.

'Dining room, *the spinis.*'

'Thank you.' Linda slipped into the room and stood quaking just inside the door.

Andreas stood at the window looking out. He turned when he heard her enter and subjected her to a long head-to-toe appraisal in which there was no mistaking the admiration.

'You can serve now,' he said to Eleni who had lingered in the doorway. He watched as Linda advanced a little further into the room.

'Would you like an *apéritif?*' he asked.

'Yes — thank you,' Linda croaked. A drink might relax her and at the same time give her something to do with her hands.

Andreas poured sherry for her as she looked admiringly round the room. Its almost severe lines were lightened by brilliant Anatolian hangings. Small sculptures and charming pieces of folk art were displayed on beautifully carved tables and cabinets. If the decoration was of Andreas Duncan's choosing, it showed exquisite and sensitive taste.

The dining-table, attractively set for two, stood near the window, and just one standard lamp challenged the dusk.

They stood side-by-side looking out into the twilit garden, to the moon trapped in the branches of the plane trees, and the mysterious silver sea. As Linda had hoped, the wine began to relax her. 'After all,' she reasoned with herself, 'to what extent am I deceiving him? I'm here under my own name. I can certainly carry out the job I undertook.' Her only deceit lay in posing as Nickie's mother, and that really was no concern of his. She had almost talked herself into a precarious peace of mind, when Andreas turned to face her, lounging gracefully against the window-frame.

'I hope your room is agreeable?'

'It's beautiful, but something smaller would have been perfectly all right.'

He shrugged slightly. 'The villa is empty most of the time. The rooms might as well be used. Has Nickie settled in?'

Linda laughed. 'Oh, perfectly. Fortunately, he makes friends easily.'

'That's good. Did you meet Katina? I'm afraid she's rather shy.'

'Yes, she did seem a little shy, but we'll soon break down the barriers. I suppose she doesn't meet a lot of people. It's very sad that she lost her parents so young.'

Andreas put down his glass. His back was half-turned to her again. 'She hasn't lost her mother,' he said. 'At least not in that sense.'

'Oh, I hadn't realised that,' Linda was confused. 'Then, why — I mean, why isn't Katina with her mother?'

Andreas turned and took Linda's glass from her hand. His face, so courteous and charming a minute before, was an icy mask.

'Because I don't consider her mother fit to look after her,' he said shortly.

★ ★ ★

Linda's shocked stare prompted him to expand his reply.

'My brother was misguided enough to prefer an English girl to a Greek. An 'emancipated woman' who thought of nothing but the fulfilment of her own selfish whims.'

Linda found her voice. 'Responsible motherhood doesn't go with nationality in my observation. English women — even emancipated ones — are usually excellent mothers, although their methods and manner may look unconventional to the outsider. Personally, I can think of few things worse than a totally selfless parent. Think of the guilt it would implant in a child!'

Andreas ignored the light note in her voice. His dark eyes were cold as they rested on her and she thought there was a hint of contempt in his expression.

'I have heard that argument advanced. A useful sop to a nagging conscience, I would imagine. We'll just have to agree to differ on the subject. I am not an outsider, however, but Katina's uncle and guardian, and I don't wish her to have a 'liberated' upbringing, with its unsettling freedoms giving her choices she isn't qualified to make.'

Linda was about to say that Katina would certainly not be capable of dealing with freedom and choice if she led an unnaturally sheltered life, but Eleni had quietly entered the room with bowls of soup, and Andreas drew out a chair for Linda to sit.

As she spooned her soup, she decided that it would be wise to let the subject drop. It seemed to engender a quite unreasonable passion in Andreas and, already, as a divorcee who was pursued by suitors in public places, she hardly qualified as a suitable companion for his niece. Moreover, the situation was far too uncannily a repetition of her own — or rather,

Julie's — position, to be comfortable. One thing was certain, if the deception, and the reason for it, came to light, she could hope for little sympathy here.

She smiled what she hoped was an appeasing smile and commented on the beauty of the house and gardens.

'Yes, it is beautiful. I only wish that I could spend more time here. My cousin Gregori should carry more weight in the business. He is twenty-four now. At that age, Robert and I were running our own departments, but then — ' he shrugged in a very Greek fashion — 'he likes to play.'

'And your other cousins? Are they all younger — or *female*?'

He looked up sharply, but her expression showed only polite interest.

'Gregori's sister, Ariadne, is twenty-two, and no, she does not, of course, play any part in the business. My uncle Dimitri has three children, Alex, Damon and Helen, but they are only in their mid-teens. So, for a time, until they are older, the workload is heavy.'

Eleni removed their soup bowls and brought in a lamb dish to which Linda did full justice. Andreas kept their glasses filled with wine which he informed her was from the villa's own vineyard and, for a time, conversation was easy and pleasant.

Fruit and various sweetmeats followed the main course and, when the meal was finished, Linda got to her feet.

'Will you please excuse me while I look in on Nickie? I promised him that I would.'

He pushed back his chair as she rose. 'Of course. Will you come back for coffee?'

'Thank you.' She put down her napkin and hurried from the room, conscious that Nickie had been alone for a long time in which he could have said, or done, anything.

When she opened her bedroom door, she found Espasia sitting under a lamp, sewing, just outside the open door of Nickie's room.

She smiled at Linda. 'He go to sleep

quick as soon as he is in bed.'

Linda tiptoed to the door and looked in at Nickie. His dark curly head was on the pillow and one chubby arm was outflung. She adjusted his cover gently.

'Thank you for sitting with him,' she whispered to the young maid.

★ ★ ★

When she re-entered the dining room, it appeared to be empty. Then she noticed that the windows to the terrace were open. Crossing to the windows, she looked out. In the faint lamplight from the room, she could just make out Andreas stretched out in a garden chair.

He got to his feet when he saw her. 'I usually take my coffee out here, if that's all right. You're not cold?'

'Not at all. This is perfect.' She sat down on another chair, a wrought-iron table between them and he poured a cup of coffee for her, Greek-style, thick, strong and sweet.

She leant back in her chair feeling incredibly relaxed. The sweet scents of the garden were intoxicating and a sensuous languor began to steal over her. Was this the sort of dangerous enchantment that Julie allowed to steal her senses? she wondered, and made a determined effort to shake it off.

Andreas was watching her. 'You are tired?' he asked in his deep voice.

'Yes, I am. I think I'll go up to bed, if you don't mind.'

'Wait just a minute or two. She will break her bonds and sail free.'

Linda looked at him, puzzled. His head was back and he was gazing skywards. Just at that moment, the moon, seemingly bigger than she had ever seen it before, cleared the top of the high trees and stood in the velvety black sky, making a broad silver highway across the sea.

Andreas gave a short laugh, as though caught in something foolish. 'The floor show's over,' he said.

He stood up and, taking her hands,

pulled her gently to her feet. The touch of his warm hands seared into hers. As she stood, looking up into his eyes, she felt an electric tension between them that she was sure he, too, was aware of.

A little huskily, he said, 'I have to leave for Athens fairly early tomorrow morning. I expect I shall be gone before you get up. In any case, I'll see you for dinner tomorrow night.'

It broke the spell. Linda said, 'Good night Mr. — Andreas.'

'Good night, Linda.'

She crossed the dining room and sped up the stairs to her room. Espasia had gone, but a low lamp burned on Linda's bedside table. She peeped in at Nickie and was pleased to see him still sleeping soundly. She hurriedly prepared for bed. The room was very warm so, with a grimace, she donned one of Julie's brief nighties, a wisp of ivory silk. Then she stretched her tired limbs beneath the cool linen sheets and considered the events of the long day.

On balance, she decided, things had

gone better than she had dared to hope. She and Nickie were safely out of England and nobody knew their whereabouts. Andreas Duncan was the unknown element. He was so totally unexpected. Shrewd and hostile, but only, she thought, hostile to the type of woman he imagined she represented.

Tomorrow she would write to Julie to reassure her that, so far, all was well. Not, she reflected, that Julie would be worried. Linda would be expected to cope as always.

Her mind, a mixture of anxiety, temporary relief, and a quite unfamiliar kind of excitement, churned feverishly for a long time before sleep finally overcame her.

* * *

She awoke before eight o'clock the next morning. She lay for a few moments savouring the comfort of the bed, before panic brought her fully awake. She stared round the bright, beautifully furnished room and wondered what she had let herself in for and how on earth she was going to carry it through. Her mouth dry with tension, she was unable to lie in bed any longer. She got out and put on Julie's wrap, pushing the shining gold curtain of hair back from her face.

She crossed to the window and knelt on the sill to look out. A soft misty sunlight touched the sea, turning it an almost opal hue. A few fishing boats were out in the bay, their sails rust-red, or sparkling white. The air was still cool and moist.

Below her, on the drive, Andreas' car stood waiting and she hung back a little to see him leave. As she did so, there was a soft knock at her door and, without thinking, she hurried to open it.

Andreas stood outside. As he looked at her, his face flooded with colour and Linda, horrified, followed his gaze, realising, too late, that she was not enveloped in her old familiar dressing-gown. All she could see was the scrap of apricot satin that clung to her, exposing her long legs and powerfully suggesting what it purported to hide. Andreas saw, too, the corn-silk cloud of hair and her face still soft with sleep.

Frantically she tried to tug the wrap around her. 'I'm sorry,' she gulped. 'I thought perhaps Eleni was bringing tea in bed.'

'You don't have to get out of bed to let her in.' He seemed to have recovered his usual self-possession. 'That would rather defeat the object — wouldn't you say?'

Linda's eyes flicked desperately round the room, but there was no other garment within reach with which to cover herself.

'I'm sorry to disturb you,' he went on coolly. 'I hoped you might be up. There are a couple of rather important reports that I would like you to type. I forgot about them last night. The drafts are on the desk in my office — Eleni will show you where it is.'

'Of course. I'll do them after breakfast.'

'Thank you.' He turned away, then turned back to where she stood outlined against the sun-bright window. 'You make a delightful sight, but Tomas sometimes has work above stairs and he is unused to such — self-expression.'

With cheeks flaming, Linda hastily shut the door on his receding back. In the long mirror, she surveyed the sight that had met his eyes and groaned aloud.

Another black mark against you, my girl, she thought as she hustled back into bed and buried her face under the pillows.

★　★　★

She was still there, recovering from the encounter, when Nickie peeped round the door of his room, then stole across to Linda's bed and snuggled up against her.

Linda put her arm round his little pyjama-clad figure and hugged him. 'Good morning, Nickie. Did you sleep well?'

102

Nickie gave an enormous yawn, then he rolled over and regarded Linda with his large brown eyes.

'Are we going home today, Lindy?'

'No, of course not, darling. We've only just got here. You haven't been to the sea yet.'

'Can we go to the sea now?'

'Some time today. I have to do some work for Mr. Duncan, but I don't expect it will take long. Perhaps you can play with Katina this morning, and the three of us can go somewhere this afternoon. Would you like that?'

'Will Mummy come today?'

'Not yet. She has to stay in England a little longer.'

Nickie appeared to accept this quite happily and Linda was relieved that a succession of baby-sitters and *au pairs* had prepared him somewhat for his present experience.

There was a second knock at the door and, although Linda stayed discreetly beneath the covers, this time it was Eleni carrying a tray on which was set freshly-baked rolls and jam, coffee, milk and fruit, which she put down on a table near the window.

Charmed by this new experience, Nickie hopped out of bed eagerly while Linda put to Eleni the plan she had suggested to Nickie.

'Yes, very nice you go to the beach in the afternoon,' Eleni agreed. 'In the morning Katina go in garden with me. She pick vegetables and herbs for dinner. Nickie go, too?'

That seemed to appeal to Nickie, and he and Linda settled down to their breakfast, sitting in the window and watching the fishing boats traversing the glittering bay. When they had finished, Linda washed and dressed herself and Nickie, and delivered him to the kitchen.

She found Eleni, Espasia and Katina all together in the big, well-equipped kitchen. She greeted them, attempting to draw Katina into conversation for a few minutes before heading for the office which Eleni pointed out to her.

Linda looked round the plainly-furnished office before locating the two reports she was to work on. She studied Andreas' firm incisive handwriting, but it told her no more about him than the bare functional office, and she sat down at the desk and read the reports through carefully to make sure that she understood what was required. They were quite complex, with a good many statistical tables and estimates, and Linda's blood ran cold at the thought of Julie struggling with them, but Andreas' instructions were clear and, in a little over two hours, she had finished, well pleased with the job she had done, and was clearing away her work.

She returned to the kitchen to find Eleni preparing lunch. She looked up with a smile when she saw Linda and nodded towards the back door. Linda went out to the patio at the back of the house where Nickie and Katina were playing some absorbing game, watched over by Espasia.

The children ran to greet Linda

eagerly and took her on a conducted tour of the extensive garden at the back of the villa. A network of paths beneath trellises smothered in sweet-smelling early roses divided the garden, disclosing here a private arbour with a rustic seat, there a grove of fruit trees — orange, lemon, peach and fig, a turquoise-bright swimming-pool surrounded by smart pool furniture, an extensive vegetable garden and, farthest from the house, up the hill, the vineyard. It seemed to Linda a place of total enchantment and she understood Andreas' love for the villa.

★ ★ ★

When they returned to the house, Eleni had set a table out on the patio in the shade of a large fig tree and, with Tomas hailed from his work, they all sat down to lunch. After lunch, the two children rested on their beds for an hour while Eleni cleared away. When they came down, Linda was ready; a towel and a paperback novel, two trowels and plant pots, begged from Tomas to do duty as buckets and spades, all packed in a straw bag provided by Eleni.

Tomas escorted them across the front lawn to the lane they had driven down the previous evening, and pointed out the track that led to the cove, cautioning her that, although the water appeared calm, there were sometimes tricky tides and she was to be careful.

There was no need for the warning. Linda was only too conscious of having responsibility for Andreas' cherished ward — to say nothing of Nickie, who was a bold and adventurous child.

She followed the narrow path through the heath-like *maquis* of juniper, broom and spurge, until they emerged at an exquisite little beach, the water lapping up the silver sand.

'Oh, Nickie,' Linda exclaimed in delight. 'Isn't this heavenly?'

She settled herself in the shade of the Aleppo pines that fringed the top of the beach. Nickie and Katina took off their shoes, Linda tucked Katina's elaborate dress into her knickers, and the two children scampered down the beach to the water's edge. Wishing fervently that she had a swimsuit with her, Linda put on her sunglasses, picked up her book and prepared to do guard duty.

It was a thoroughly enjoyable afternoon. The children paddled and floated scraps of wood for 'boats' and, when Linda called them to come out, they had a sand-castle competition. The competition was diplomatically declared a draw and, at four-thirty, they trailed, tired but happy, back to the villa.

Eleni tut-tutted a little over Katina's crumpled dress, but was obviously pleased to see the child so happy. After they had washed, she served fresh lemonade and delicious little cakes dripping with honey. Then Linda took the children into the sitting room, where they curled up happily beside her on the big settee while she read to them from the picture-books she had brought with her to amuse Nickie.

Katina was particularly enchanted at being read to, as though it was a pastime she was quite unfamiliar with. The simply-captioned picture-books were a useful aid to her English.

From five o'clock onwards, Linda realised that she was waiting for Andreas' return with a mixture of dread and pleasure but, just after six o'clock, it was Katina's sharp ears that heard his car on the drive. She jumped up and ran out into the hall and Linda heard her chattering excitedly in Greek for some moments. Noting that her own name was frequently repeated, she hoped she was getting a good Press.

Then Andreas appeared in the doorway, dragged along by his eager niece. At the sight of him, so vital and dynamic, Linda's heart turned over. She started to get up from the depth of the settee, but Andreas flopped down, rather wearily, beside her, pulling Katina on to his knees.

'Well, you're certainly a hit!' he said.

'I've never heard Katina so animated. You've been to the beach, I hear.'

'I hope it was all right to take the children?'

'Of course. I know you'll be careful. It looks smooth and calm, but underneath there are dangerous currents.' He cocked a sardonic brow at her and she sensed that he was not speaking solely of the sea. Then he leant back and sighed. 'Ah, it's good to be home. The Athens traffic gets more diabolical every day.'

The four of them chatted for a few minutes, then Andreas excused himself to go and shower and change. After a while, he returned, more casually dressed in a fine wool sweater and cotton trousers.

'I've looked over your typing in the office,' he said. 'It's first-rate.'

Linda flushed. 'I'm glad it was satisfactory.'

Katina climbed on Andreas' knee and read to him the words she had learned from the English books until it was time for Espasia to take the children away for their evening meal.

Left alone with Andreas, Linda was momentarily overwhelmed with shyness, but he put her at her ease, talking casually of the events of his day in Athens. During dinner the relaxed conversation continued. They sat long over the meal, exchanging experiences and opinions, then went for a walk along the beach where Andreas pointed out the distant villages, pin-pointed by little clusters of lights, and the brilliant floodlights of the night fishing-boats. When, at bedtime, Linda said good night and took her leave in a confused haze of happiness, it was almost with reluctance.

4

The following morning was a Sunday and her first thought on waking was that she might have a whole day of Andreas' company. She groaned shame-facedly and rolled on to her stomach. To think that only forty-eight hours ago she had wanted nothing but to keep out of his way for the whole three months.

A tap on her door announced the arrival of Eleni, accompanied by Katina, who was wearing her usual elaborate dress and knee-length socks. Already Linda could feel the warmth of the sun's rays slanting into her room, a promise of the heat that would come later.

As Eleni set her breakfast-tray down on the table in the window, she said, 'Eleni, doesn't Katina have any casual clothes? Clothes to play in?'

The housekeeper looked surprised.

'Mr. Andreas buy Katina's clothes.'

'Oh, her dresses are beautiful,' Linda said swiftly. 'I just thought that she must be rather hot in them. And she got so grubby on the beach yesterday. They must be hard to wash and iron.'

'I don't mind to wash and iron,' Eleni said stubbornly. 'Is my job.'

'I know you don't mind,' Linda said. 'And I shouldn't have interfered. I thought Katina would be more comfortable in T-shirts and — perhaps — shorts. The sort of thing Nickie wears.'

Katina had now taken an interest in the conversation. 'I like Nickie's clothes. Can I not have T-shorts, Eleni?'

'Nickie has some things that are far too big for him. Could Katina try them on, just to play in this morning? She could put her lovely dress on for lunch.'

While Eleni hesitated, Nickie who had emerged, yawning sleepily, from his little bedroom, instantly took a short-cut through the discussion, pulling open a drawer and recklessly distributing his wardrobe.

Linda sorted out a lemon-yellow pair of shorts and a yellow-and-white striped T-shirt that Julie had bought for the trip. Nickie was a big child for his age and Katina small for hers, and Julie had bought a very generous size.

'These, perhaps?' Linda suggested tentatively, holding the garments up for Eleni's approval.

Eleni still looked far from convinced, but Katina had hastily pulled off her dress, followed, Linda noted, by an almost equally elaborate petticoat, and was scrambling into the proffered clothes.

It was a transformation. The clothes fitted snugly and the yellow was just the right shade for Katina's rather sallow colouring. With swift experienced fingers, Linda swirled the child's heavy curls into a trim knot on the top of her head.

A hint of doubt still touched Eleni's smile of approval. 'Is very nice, but what Mr. Andreas say?'

Linda swallowed nervously. That

thought had occurred to her. 'Don't worry. I'm sure he'll agree that these things are more suitable for play. In any case, I'll tell him it was my idea.'

Eleni returned to her kitchen, leaving Katina behind, pirouetting in front of the large mirror, while Linda and Nickie got on with their breakfast.

When they had finished, she washed and dressed Nickie and herself, putting on a simple, full-skirted dress in apple-green cotton and, with a child on either hand, led the way out to the garden.

★ ★ ★

It was nearly lunchtime before Andreas appeared. Linda had spent a pleasant morning lazing beside the pool with a book, occasionally joining the children in their seemingly tireless game of hide-and-seek among the nooks and crannies of a garden that was made for such a pastime.

She sensed a dark shadow looming

over her as she reclined back in her chair and put a hand up to screen her eyes from the sun. Andreas stood before her, wearing a brief white towelling robe that showed off his tanned, muscular legs.

Feeling oddly vulnerable, sprawled below him, she jerked quickly upright but, with a smile, he gestured her to relax.

'Good morning. There's just time for a dip before lunch. Won't you join me?'

Linda shook her head regretfully. 'I'm afraid I forgot to pack a swimsuit.'

'That won't do! I'll ring my cousin in Athens during the week and ask her to pick one out for you.'

'That's very kind of you. I was sorry not to have one on the beach yesterday.'

He moved away from her to the other end of the pool, dropped his robe at his feet and, through eyes half-closed against the sun, Linda briefly admired his lithe, tautly-muscled body before he clove the water in a neat dive.

He circled the pool in a lazy crawl,

the water drops glistening on his brown skin and in his thick dark hair, and Linda felt something stir within her at the controlled sensuality of his movements.

After a few minutes, he pulled himself up out of the water to sit on the pool's edge beside her.

'Where are the children?'

'They're playing behind the trellis. I can hear their voices.'

'Ah, yes.' He turned to look in the direction of the trellis just as Nickie and Katina catapulted into view. Katina had added grubby bare feet and a grimy streak across her nose to her casual appearance, and Linda's heart sank as a thunderous expression appeared on Andreas' face.

'Nickie, I recognise, but who is this other urchin?'

Linda began a stumbling explanation, but Katina had hurtled across the patio and into her uncle's arms.

'It's me, Katina!' she shouted, her eyes shining.

Andreas hugged the child to his wet chest, and turned to Linda whose apologia was feebly petering out. The long slow look he gave her was impossible to fathom, but most of the anger seemed to have been diffused from it.

'I'm sorry if you disapprove,' she finished lamely.

He made no response, but said to Katina, 'Well, some water seems to be in order!' He slid off the edge of the pool with her up in his arms, until the water reached above her knees.

Katina shrieked ecstatically, Nickie clamoured to join them, and the scene ended with Andreas carrying a child on each arm, immersing them deeper and deeper until both were thoroughly soaked.

The rest of the day was equally enjoyable. After lunch the children rested and Linda did an hour's typing in the office while Andreas worked alongside her. Then they all walked on the beach and, after the children had been put to bed, dined together, then played records until it was time for Linda to retire.

★ ★ ★

The next week, with minor changes, followed the pattern that had been established. Andreas left early in the morning for Athens, leaving varying amounts of work for Linda. Sometimes she was finished in half-an-hour, sometimes it was hard going for three hours. Always he expressed appreciation of the work she had done.

She found that, more and more, she was longing for his return from Athens in the evenings. She grew restless if he was later than usual, her imagination tormenting her with what he might be doing.

Then, when he did arrive, there was the intimate, almost domestic routine of dinner together, coffee in the fragrant moonlit garden, listening to music and a late stroll on the beach. But always a barely submerged tension between them — that she was sure he felt, too — undermined any comfortable suggestion of domesticity. And, when they parted to go to their rooms at night, the reluctance, she was equally sure, was mutual.

In her free time, she took the children to the beach and explored the country round about. Katina's English had advanced by leaps and bounds. She had become very attached to Linda and was far more clinging than Nickie who appeared to have almost forgotten his mother.

It concerned Linda that the little girl was pinning so much importance to a relationship that must be brief and would only bring her more heartache. She wondered how much contact Katina had with her mother and wished that she had the courage to broach the subject with Andreas.

Matters were brought to a head on the Thursday afternoon as Linda read a story to the children in which a birthday featured.

'My birthday is next week!' Katina announced. 'I am six!'

'Is it really, darling?' said Linda. 'Do you know what day?'

'I think — Friday,' Katina responded doubtfully.

'Then I must find out. Perhaps we can have a little party,' Linda said. 'What do you want most for your birthday?'

Katina thought for a moment. 'I want *Mamá* to come,' she said.

Linda was deeply moved, but there were no promises she could give on that score, so she hugged the little girl wordlessly, determined, now, to put her qualms aside and speak to Andreas. Perhaps the trust and respect that she believed he now had for her would allow her to venture into an area which seemed to arouse irrational anger in him.

She could not have been more wrong. Perhaps her timing was off, Andreas had seemed more than usually exhausted when he arrived back from the city, but as soon as she brought the subject round to Katina, as they sat down to dinner, a wariness crept into his eyes.

She had begun by reminding him of the approaching birthday, to which he replied that he had not forgotten it and that a present was being taken care of.

'I wondered what to give her myself,' Linda said.

'Rather difficult — she has practically everything.'

Linda felt a rush of blood to her cheeks. Katina was not her idea of a child who had everything.

Before she could stop herself, she said, 'She wants her mother to come for her birthday.'

Andreas put down his fork carefully.

'She wants *what*?' he said, and the fact that his voice was quiet made it somehow more alarming.

Linda licked her lips nervously. 'She said that she would like her mother to come,' she repeated in a voice that trembled slightly.

Andreas picked up his fork and concentrated on his plate. 'That is out of the question,' he said.

Everything in Linda counselled her to let the matter drop but, gathering her courage in both hands, she persisted, 'Why is it out of the question?'

'That is hardly your business, is it? May I ask you *not* to meddle in my private family affairs?'

'I was not meddling — '

'Do you deny you put this idea into Katina's head?'

'Of course I deny it!' Linda protested hotly. 'It's hardly an unnatural idea that someone would need to suggest to her. It's the most natural thing in the world.'

'Very possibly, but it's a relationship that I have been doing my utmost to discourage.' Seeing the shock in her face, he raised his voice. 'Don't try to make me feel a brute! In what way is Nickie's situation different to Katina's? You have deprived him of a father — no doubt for your own selfish ends. I don't know — I haven't pried into your affairs.'

The counter accusation took the wind out of Linda's sails. She opened her mouth to deny the unjust charge, but obviously no defence was possible.

Hot tears sprang to her eyes and a lump rose in her throat. She pushed her plate miserably away from her.

Andreas' expression softened slightly. 'I'm sorry that we've had this disagreement. I've been delighted at the way you've brought Katina out. Some small things I may not agree with, but her happiness has undermined any disapproval. But in this matter I will not be crossed. You are interfering in a situation you know nothing about.'

It was on the tip of Linda's tongue to protest once more that she hadn't been interfering, but she hadn't the heart for it. In a voice that was rough with unshed tears she said, 'It was just that — I was afraid she was getting too fond of me.'

Andreas looked at the figure opposite

him. The candlelight made a bright halo of her golden hair, her eyes were suspiciously bright, and there was an unaccustomed downward droop to her soft mouth.

When he spoke, his own voice sounded rough. 'You make it too easy,' he said.

Linda's cheeks flamed again, but at that moment Eleni entered the room. She looked curiously from one to the other of them, sensing the tense atmosphere, before serving their dessert and withdrawing once more.

After the interruption they ate in silence for a few minutes, before Andreas said in a placatory tone, 'My two cousins are arriving on Saturday morning for the weekend. They will be bringing Katina's presents — and, I hope, a swimsuit for you.'

'Is that the older two?'

'Yes, Gregori and Ariadne. They're consumed with curiosity about you.'

Linda's heart missed a beat. Too much curiosity was something she felt she could easily do without. But she merely said steadily, 'I'll be interested to meet them.'

'I was hoping that the younger three would come as well, to make a little celebration for Katina, but they're not free. But we must arrange a beach picnic, or something of the sort, although I should warn you that Gregori will only have one pastime in mind.'

'Oh?' She looked at him questioningly.

'You, my dear Linda. Gregori is a very impressionable young man. Oh, I'm sure that you will be able to deal with him, but I wouldn't advise any appearance in scanty underwear!'

'That really isn't a regular habit of mine!' Linda snapped and, once again, the atmosphere was cool and hostile between them.

This time it showed no signs of recovering and Linda excused herself from the table before the coffee arrived, saying that she had letters to write.

She went up to her room in a mood both unhappy and apprehensive. The scene with Andreas over Katina had shaken her deeply. She had been so nearly won over by his courtesy and apparent sensitivity in the previous week, that she had almost forgotten this cruel side of his nature. And the imminent arrival of his two cousins filled her with unease, particularly as Andreas had warned her that Gregori was certain to take an interest in her.

She heaved a sigh and, getting out her writing case, prepared to write a letter to Julie begging her once again to do her utmost to expedite matters and allow her to have done with the Villa Minerva and everyone connected with it.

* * *

It didn't take long after the arrival of the cousins, the following morning, for Linda to realise that her worst fears were justified. Not only Gregori, but his sister, too, displayed a deep interest in her presence at the villa.

The reason for Ariadne's interest was obvious from the moment of her arrival. A sports car had roared up the drive and, on hearing it, Linda looked out of her bedroom window in time to see the two young people alight from it.

They were a matching pair. Darkly beautiful with thick curling black hair, golden tanned skins and big dark eyes. The young man wore tight-fitting trousers in cream denim and a light-blue sweat shirt, the girl a white dress and white strappy sandals. Sunglasses were pushed up over her shining dark hair.

As Linda watched, Andreas came out of the house and the girl ran into his arms. She kissed him long and full on the mouth — no cousin's kiss — and Linda felt a stab at her heart. Andreas embraced his male cousin. Then the three of them disappeared from view into the house.

Linda lingered in her room, distressed by the warmth of Ariadne's greeting, and the strength of her own reaction to it. Then the sound of Nickie's voice, chattering uninhibitedly to the new arrivals, roused her and, fearing an innocent indiscretion on his part, she hastened downstairs.

She entered the sitting room to find Nickie and Katina vying for the attention of Ariadne Katrakis who was sprawled on a settee displaying a good deal of leg and looking rather bored.

Andreas and Gregori were talking together by the window. They turned to look at Linda as she came in. She had put on a yellow cotton dress with a close-fitting bodice and full skirt. Gregori Katrakis allowed his gaze to run slowly and appreciatively over her.

'Well — ' he murmured at last. 'There's no need to wonder any longer where you've been keeping yourself these last few evenings, Andreas, you wicked old devil!' He sauntered across to Linda. His eyes had never left her and she flushed before his bold appraisal.

'Linda,' Andreas said, and he, too, was watching her closely. 'These are my cousins, Ariadne and Gregori. My secretary — Linda Blair.'

'Secretary?' Gregori's tone was openly scoffing. He took Linda's hand. 'It was my impression that the office was well supplied with secretaries — or are all those charming creatures just running around for my benefit?'

'No, they're not,' Andreas retorted. 'Although you — and they — appear to think so. However, whatever other talents they may have, none of them, as far as I am aware, can transcribe and type acceptable English.'

'So you brought Linda over from the London office? Funny, I never see anything like her when I'm over there.'

'Linda didn't work for us in London.'

'So — where you find her?' Ariadne had sat up and was taking an interest. Her accent was much stronger than her brother's and, whether intentional or not, her delivery sounded distinctly unfriendly.

With a determined tug, Linda regained possession of her hand. 'I answered a newspaper advertisement, Miss Katrakis,' she said.

'You don't know Andreas before?' Ariadne asked, her eyes narrowed.

'Not until we met at the airport.'

★　★　★

The Greek girl's eyes flicked to Nickie. 'He your little boy?'

'Yes — yes, he is,' Linda muttered, praying that Nickie wouldn't choose this moment to contradict her.

Ariadne subjected Nickie to a more prolonged appraisal. 'He looks like Greek boy,' she said flatly.

Gregori threw back his head, displaying dazzling white teeth, and crowed with laughter. 'My dear sister, what are you suggesting?'

Linda felt the hot blush rushing to her cheeks. 'Nickie is not Greek,' she managed to get out.

'And you are very bad-mannered,' Andreas said to his cousins. To Linda's surprise, he took her hand and gave it a friendly squeeze. 'Linda — who was a complete stranger to me — is here as the result of a plot cooked up between my father and Mrs. Mac. She is bringing order to the chaotic backlog of my English correspondence and, at the same time, she is helping Katina with her English — again very efficiently.'

Warmed by his support, Linda shot him a look of gratitude that was not lost on Ariadne.

Sulkily, the Greek girl said, 'How long she stay?'

'She stay just as long as I say,' Andreas mimicked. 'Good grief, what did they teach you at that expensive school? You sound as though you need Linda's services.'

Ariadne uncoiled herself from the settee. Crossing to Andreas, she wound her arms around his neck and, standing on tiptoe, dropped a light kiss on his ear.

'They teach me to be a good Greek wife, Andreas, darling,' she cooed.

Andreas took hold of her arms and freed himself firmly.

'I'm very glad to hear it. But it's just possible that your husband will require you to converse a little beyond kindergarten level.'

Not wishing to make an enemy of the other girl, Linda attempted to relieve the situation. 'Miss Katrakis' English is a lot better than my Greek,' she said lightly.

She was rewarded by Andreas rounding on her. His black brows drew together in exasperation. 'But you, my dear Linda, have had only a few days' exposure to Greek — not several years of expensive tuition. And, whether we like it or not, it is English, and not Greek, that is now the *lingua franca* of the civilised world.'

There was a brief strained silence, broken by Nickie. 'Lindy, that man

133

came in a smashing car. Look!' He rushed at her and dragged her to the window from where she could see the Katrakis cousins' car. 'Look, Lindy, isn't it *great*?'

Gregori strolled across to join them. 'Your little son likes cars?' His warm brown eyes gazed appreciatively into hers. 'Perhaps you would like to come for a run?'

'Yes, yes!' Nickie clamoured excitedly. 'Say yes, Lindy!'

'Yes, yes!' Katina joined in, not quite sure what was on offer, but positive that it would be agreeable.

'I'm sure the children would enjoy that,' Linda said demurely, and Gregori endeavoured to hide his irritation before Andreas' sardonic grin.

Ariadne was still regarding Linda as though trying to sum up her position in the house. Apparently deciding to postpone the problem, she shrugged lightly. 'I go for a swim before lunch. Will you swim with me, Andreas?'

'Good idea. Let's all have a swim. I

hope you remembered the swimsuit for Linda.'

Ariadne gasped in dismay, putting a hand to her mouth and widening her eyes.

'Oh, Andreas, I'm so sorry! It just slip my mind. I have such a busy week.'

It was the most obvious performance Linda had seen in her life and she couldn't believe that Andreas didn't see through it. Certainly he was looking very angry.

'Ariadne, that's really maddening! Linda has been waiting for a dip all week.'

The enormous eyes grew misty with tears. 'I'm very sorry, Andreas — '

'Don't apologise to me! Apologise to Miss Blair. Haven't you got one you could lend her?'

'I just bring one,' Ariadne whispered in a tiny voice.

'It's all right, really,' Linda said swiftly. 'I have to keep an eye on the children, anyway.'

Andreas still looked unmollified, but

only said, 'What about you, Gregori?'

Gregori grinned. 'Oh, I'll keep an eye on Linda.'

Andreas hesitated, as though he might change his mind, but Ariadne linked his arm firmly and towed him from the room.

★　★　★

'Such a handsome pair,' Gregori observed. 'They are well-suited, do you not think?'

Linda looked at him uncertainly. To her, Andreas and Ariadne appeared far from well-suited. Andreas was a cultivated and intelligent man of the world. As far as she could tell, on very brief acquaintance, Ariadne was nothing but a spoilt and silly little flirt, and probably, she decided unfairly, by no means the innocent that Andreas might believe.

'You don't agree?' Gregori persisted, still watching her closely. 'But Andreas is a handsome brute, and my sister is very pretty, no?'

'Yes, she is. Very pretty.' Linda was spared comment on the first part of the equation when Nickie erupted once again. 'Lindy, can we go for a ride in the man's car?'

'Nickie, this is Mr. Katrakis — don't call him 'the man'.' Linda glanced at Gregori apologetically. 'I'm sorry, he's a little excited — '

'He'd better call me Gregori. Mr. Katrakis is a bit of a mouthful. Well, how about it? We can have a run up the coast as far as Kastri, and be back in time for lunch.'

Linda hesitated, but she could see no reason why she should refuse the invitation, particularly in the face of the children's excitement. She helped Katina and Nickie into the back seat of the car, instructing them not to stand up, and climbed in herself.

Gregori whirled the car round in a tight half-circle and accelerated down the drive, and Linda put a restraining arm behind her to secure the children.

Gregori turned to grin at her. 'You dislike speed?'

'Not at all. I'm just concerned for the children.'

'They love it!'

Looking at Nickie and Katina's rapt faces, Linda could see that he was right. 'All the same,' she retorted, 'I've no desire to see them flying over the side.'

He smiled, but reduced speed fractionally, and Linda had time to look around her. To her left, the land sloped steadily up from the sea, as tawny as an old lion with its cover of olive trees and thick-carpeting asphodel. To their right was a rocky promontory clustered with pines. Through the trees, Linda caught glimpses of the azure sea, studded with small craft and, at its edge, the tantalising flash of a succession of tiny golden beaches.

They passed a few small villas, flanked by their own lemon groves, and more numerous simple cottages, some vine-covered, some sheltered by a huge fig tree, but all freshly white-washed and fronted by a well-hoed kitchen garden.

There was little sign of life. In an occasional garden, a black-clad figure paused in his labour to look up at the passing car. A few goats scrubbed about the foothills. A small boy walked a donkey along the roadside, tapping half-heartedly with a stick at its ancient rump.

In a little over ten minutes, both dwellings and inhabitants suddenly grew more numerous. They passed a decrepit filling-station and a shack-like taverna with a group of old men seated outside, intent on some game. A row of cottages reached out from the town, with women gossiping in the gardens, and children and dogs scampering in and out of doors.

★ ★ ★

Gregori turned a corner and stopped. The town was little more than a score of houses grouped round a central

139

square. There was a well in the centre of the square, beneath a plane tree, and the women waiting with their jugs made an almost biblical scene.

'Kastri!' Gregori announced with a flourish.

Linda got out of the car and helped Nickie and Katina down. She looked around her and realised that she was the focus of friendly attention. The women smiled warmly, taking in every detail of her appearance. A number of curious children appeared from nowhere and shyly drew nearer.

'*Kaliméra*,' Gregori called, waving a greeting. His manner, Linda thought, was that of a feudal lord with his peasants.

A number of scrawny hens picking over the beaten earth of the square attracted the attention of Nickie. A novelty to him, their squawking and flapping at his cautious approach enchanted him and he began to make little runs at them, followed by Katina, and then the village children.

Gregori took Linda's arm and, pulling her closer to him, started to tour the square. There was little, individually, of particular charm, the town was an entity that didn't break down into components. It was no showplace, but a living, working, community, utterly right in its setting.

Some of the cottages were larger, or better-tended, than others. One served as a shop and, as the letterbox on the wall outside indicated, as the post-office, also. Peeping in, Linda saw sacks of various dry goods on the floor. Spades and forks, hoes, rakes and sieves were propped in the doorway.

They completed their circuit of the square and arrived at the *kafenion*, a big, white-walled room open to the street, with a long counter stacked with cups and glasses. A dozen men, mainly elderly, sat on benches around the wall drinking coffee. Outside in the sunshine, in the shade of a plane tree, two once-smart tables surrounded by little chairs had been placed.

Gregori settled Linda and the children at one of the tables and, in a moment, a heavily-moustached man came out to serve them.

Gregori ordered coffee for Linda and himself, and pressed fruit juice for the children.

'They're all men,' Linda said, looking into the *kafenion*. 'In an English coffee shop, most of the patrons would be women.'

'Greek women don't have leisure time to spend drinking coffee,' Gregori said. 'Although, you'll observe that none of the ladies at the well has moved a muscle — except for their tongues — since our arrival.'

The coffee arrived, strong and sweet, in tiny cups, with a glass of water to follow and Linda sat back in her chair, enjoying the tableau before her, as she sipped it.

Only Gregori's bold, intense scrutiny, so like those that she'd suffered from the Mancini brothers, spoiled her enjoyment of the moment. He hitched his chair nearer hers and his fingers twisted a tendril of hair that curled at the nape of her neck.

'Tell me, Linda,' he asked. 'Where is your husband? What sort of man is he who lets you live with another man?'

* * *

Linda jerked her head away from his hand. 'I'm not answerable to any man. And I'm not 'living with' your cousin in that sense of the word, as you perfectly well know.'

'No, to be honest, I can't see Andreas going in for that sort of thing,' Gregori conceded. 'His standards are too high. Probably keeping himself pure for the mother of his children!'

'He has never been married?' Linda couldn't resist asking. She tried to make the question casual, knowing it was impossible with a shrewd customer like Gregori.

His eyes read her mercilessly, but he only said, 'No. If Andreas had ever been

143

married, you can bet he would still be married. Andreas does not believe in failure — in marriage, or anything else. And particularly with the example of Robert and Susan.'

'Susan?' Linda glanced at Katina, but she had finished her drink and was absorbed in a game of hide-and-seek with Nickie. 'Katina's mother?'

'That's right. But if Robert hadn't been killed, there would almost certainly have been a divorce. Andreas was in favour of it in their case.'

'What on earth had it got to do with Andreas?'

Gregori seemed surprised at her warmth. 'Why — it's important to the company. It's a big business, a great deal of money is involved. It is not unreasonable.' His hot brown eyes looked suggestively into hers. 'Suppose a Katrakis — or a Duncan — wife was unfaithful and produced a child — an heir to this wealth — who was, in fact, not a Katrakis at all.'

'Dreadful!' Linda said drily. 'And

Andreas thought this was a possibility with Susan?'

'Oh, I don't go so far as that! But he never approved of her.'

'What had he got against her?'

'Well, she was — as you say in England — flighty. She liked parties, having a good time — '

'But, Gregori,' Linda put in sweetly, 'don't you like parties and having a good time?'

Gregori looked almost comically shocked. 'But she was a woman. A married woman.'

Linda smiled grimly. 'And English.'

'That didn't help. Andreas' experience of English girls doesn't endear them to him.'

'Really?' Linda took a sip of water to cleanse her palate. 'Has he had much experience of English women?'

'I doubt it. But he has eyes. In the summer these beaches are full of them, camping with their boy friends.' He ogled her again. 'One small tent between them — you understand? The nightspots of Athens are crowded with them, drinking too much, picking up men. It horrifies him.'

It was a little shocking to Linda and certainly not the sort of conduct she went in for herself, but she felt herself obscurely compelled to defend her countrywomen.

'He's just jumping to conclusions. Everyone lets off steam a little on holiday after working hard for fifty weeks of the year. And as for the campers — how does he know they're not married?'

'I just tell you his feelings. He is not a tolerant man.'

'I never heard anything so unreasonable,' Linda snapped. She picked up her shoulder-bag, preparatory to leaving.

Gregori caught at her wrists, holding them firmly. 'But why are you so cross? Andreas treats you with courtesy. You are adequately paid, surely?' He watched her closely with knowing eyes. 'What else matters?'

What else indeed? Why were tears

pricking at the back of her eyes? 'Because I want him to like me — to respect me,' she admitted to herself. She tilted her chin. 'You're right — it doesn't matter. The terms of the job are excellent.'

She snatched her wrists away, called up the children and headed for the car.

Gregori hurried after her. 'Why do we waste the whole time talking of Andreas? I am not like him. Me, I am broad-minded. I enjoy very much the company of English women — their friends, their lack of inhibitions — '

'Which you take advantage of, only to despise them afterwards!' Linda flashed. She helped the children into the car, then got in herself, her profile averted. Gregori jumped into the driver's seat, slamming the door with a muttered oath, and they drove back to the Villa Minerva in a hostile silence.

★   ★   ★

But when they arrived, Gregori seemed to have recovered his good spirits.

147

There was no savour for him in too easy a kill. The prey that thwarted him for a time was the one that excited him. He carried Nickie on his shoulder beneath the portico arch to the back of the house, Linda and Katina following behind.

A buffet lunch was waiting on a table near the pool. Ariadne was reclining in a lounger, wearing a tiny bikini and, just as they arrived, Andreas came out through the French windows, clad in brief white shorts and a blue sweat shirt. He took in the picture they presented with a slight sardonic lift of an eyebrow.

'We waited lunch for you,' he said. 'Did you enjoy yourselves?'

'Terrific!' Gregori exclaimed, with more enthusiasm, Linda felt, than the excursion warranted. 'I think I'll stay on for a few days. I could do with a break from the city.'

'You've just got back to the city after your mountain trip,' Andreas said. 'And how would Ariadne get back to Athens?'

'She can drive in with you on Monday morning.'

There was a silence while they helped themselves from the assortment of dishes. Andreas was looking in a black mood and it occurred to Linda that he probably suspected her of persuading Gregori to extend his stay at the villa.

As he filled their wine glasses, he said, 'I'm sorry, but you can't be spared, Gregori.'

Gregori seemed about to protest, but saw from Andreas' expression that he was immovable. He made a grimace and put his lips against Linda's ear. In a whisper, audible to all the table, he said, 'Never mind. I'll be back next weekend and we'll have some fun.'

Linda jerked her head away and concentrated on helping Nickie with his lunch.

As soon as lunch was over, she took Nickie up to his room for a nap and lay down on her own bed with a book. It seemed safer to stay out of the way for a while. It appeared to annoy Andreas to

see her spending time with Gregori —
perhaps he feared another member of
his family falling victim to a scheming
Englishwoman.

As for Ariadne, if she spent much
time in that young woman's company,
she would find it hard to keep her
temper. Could she really be being
groomed as a wife for Andreas? In
material ways she might be perfect, the
same background, even the same
family, but would her apparently
limited, childish character really satisfy
him? On the other hand, maybe she was
exactly what he was looking for — the
raw material for a perfect wife to be
moulded completely to his ways.

She heaved a sigh and, picking up her
book, tried to absorb herself in it while
Nickie slept. When she heard him stir-
ring, she took him quietly downstairs
and out through the front door, unseen
by the family around the pool, and they
went for a walk along the beach.

★ ★ ★

They got back just as Eleni was carrying coffee and cakes out to the poolside-table. Ariadne and Gregori were stretched out on loungers wearing swimsuits. There was no sign of Andreas.

Linda accepted the cup of coffee Eleni poured for her, supplied Nickie with orange juice and cake, and sat down in the shade of an oleander tree. To her annoyance, Gregori immediately dragged his sunbed across the terrace to recline at her feet, gazing up at her in an embarrassing fashion.

'Where have you been?' he demanded petulantly. 'I search and search for you.'

'I took Nickie for a walk on the beach.'

'But we have such a short time together. Tomorrow I must leave. Why do you avoid me? I know! After dinner we will drive to Vikos and go dancing.'

'I don't think so, thank you. I have to listen for Nickie.'

'But there are servants!'

'The servants aren't paid to look after him.'

151

'Oh, Eleni won't mind. I'll ask her — she'll do anything for me. Just for an hour or two — '

'No, I really don't think so — '

'Give it a rest, Gregori. The girl said 'no'.'

They both jumped at the quiet voice behind them and, turning swiftly, Linda saw, on the other side of the thick, clustering oleander bushes, Andreas sitting at a small table laden with papers.

'You're not working here!' Gregori exclaimed aghast.

'Someone has to,' Andreas said shortly. 'So I would appreciate it if you would conduct your pursuit of Miss Blair elsewhere.'

Linda's cheeks flamed, but Gregori was irrepressible.

'Then we will have our dance here! I left some records here and the lights are still in the trees from Ariadne's birthday party. I'll bet your Mama likes to dance, doesn't she, Nickie?'

A little bewildered at the introduction of his mother, Nickie, nevertheless, responded with enthusiasm. 'Oh, yes. She goes out dancing all the time.'

Linda closed her eyes in mortification, even before she heard Andreas' dry voice from behind his leafy screen. 'How very dull it must have been here for your mother. Gregori must certainly organise some entertainment for her.'

Nickie looked even more bewildered at this new connection of his mother with the Villa Minerva. He opened his mouth to respond, but Linda swiftly wet her handkerchief in the pool and wiped it over his sticky face, until only his puzzled brown eyes were visible.

As soon as possible she whisked him indoors, where he discovered Katina 'helping' in the kitchen, then went up to her room.

She was called to the dinner-table at seven o'clock, an hour earlier than usual, so that, as a special treat, the two children could eat with the family. Linda was heartily glad of their presence, as in talking with them and helping Nickie with his meal, she was to some extent insulated from Gregori's determined flirting, and the misery of watching Ariadne, radiant in rose-coloured chiffon, whispering so intimately with Andreas.

She herself had put on the dressiest outfit she could muster. A Grecian-style dress of white silk jersey, lent to her by Julie, it showed off her figure to perfection. In the shining pleats of her hair she had secured tiny sprigs of orange blossom. She was conscious of looking her best, and, once or twice, her eyes risking a glance at Andreas, caught his, warmly appreciative, resting on her.

★   ★   ★

The moment they had finished eating, Gregori rushed outside into the garden. At the flick of a switch, the flower-laden borders, arbours and terraces were turned into a fairyland as scores of tiny coloured lights sprung up in the trees.

Then he switched on the music centre, which he had moved to the terrace door and Greek music flooded out over the garden. He extended his arms, not to either of the women, but to Andreas, who shook his head, laughing. Then Tomas emerged from the shadowy garden beyond the reach of the lights and, resting his arm across Gregori's shoulder, swept into the famous *chassapiko* dance, their knees bending and stretching, their fingers snapping to the rhythm of the plaintive *bouzoukia*. After a few minutes, Andreas couldn't resist its appeal, and he, too, joined the dance.

Unobserved in the candle-lit dining-room, Linda watched the men going through the ancient intricate movements. Tomas, in his working clothes, square, burly and intent, Gregori, laughing in excitement, and Andreas, perhaps most transported, his dark eyes far away, lost in the melancholy music.

The men danced on until Nickie ran out on to the terrace and was grabbed by Gregori at the end of the line, where he attempted to emulate them, snapping his fingers and kicking out his chubby legs.

The dancers collapsed in laughter and Gregori replaced the cassette with a popular dance tune. He turned to Linda and pulled her into his arms. He was warm from his exertion and, she realised belatedly, had probably drunk a good deal of wine with dinner. He crushed her to him closely and danced with her out into the shadowy garden, beyond the reach of the lights, murmuring compliments and letting his lips play over her throat and ears.

It was a situation Linda would have given anything to avoid. Over Gregori's shoulder, she watched Andreas as he talked with Tomas. Could he think she was willingly — eagerly — submitting to Gregori's embraces? His eyes seemed to be on her but, in the dim light, it was impossible to read their expression.

The music ended, but Gregori made no move to release her, laughing as she endeavoured to free herself, and finally bringing his mouth down full on hers. She began to struggle in earnest, aware that the murmur of conversation on the terrace had died. Then Gregori was jerked firmly away and Andreas stood in front of her.

'May I suggest a cool dip? The pool is that way,' he said shortly to his cousin. Then, turning to Linda, 'Would you care to dance?'

'No. Thank you.' Linda put up a trembling hand to a strand of hair that had escaped.

'Then perhaps a glass of wine.' Andreas took her arm gently and led her to a dim corner of the terrace nearer the house. He poured a glass of wine and brought it to her.

'You must forgive Gregori. The wine has gone to his head. And you embody all that Greek men find most irresistible. Blonde beauty, an independence of manner. We are easy prey.'

'I would hardly describe your cousin as the prey!'

'No, you are right,' he conceded.

'But, regrettably, we do seem to have this weakness.'

Linda leant back against the wall of the house, sipping her wine and struggling to regain her composure. Andreas lounged beside her, his foot up on a low garden wall. The heady scent of the flowers and shrubs in the warm night was overwhelming, but through it she was aware of the masculine smell of his body and his elusive expensive cologne.

★ ★ ★

In the middle of the terrace, Espasia and the two children were revolving, hands linked, in a solemn dance of their own devising. Near them, Gregori and Ariadne danced together sulkily. Andreas took the almost empty glass from her fingers.

'Come. Everyone dances but us,' he said firmly.

He drew her into his arms and she experienced a rush of emotions that shocked and alarmed her. Her heart pounded in her throat and her legs felt weak. He did not hold her close, as Gregori had done — their bodies did not touch — but there was an electric tension in the tiny space between them and Linda's whole body ached to leap it.

She was holding herself rigid, striving to hang on to her self-possession, and she thought that Andreas was doing the same. Then, suddenly, he gave a little grunt and pulled her close against him.

For a few minutes they danced together in perfect harmony, their bodies moving as one to the sentimental music, then his breath came rough and uneven, and he lowered his head to her golden crown of hair.

'Oh, I want him so,' Linda thought desperately.

Then, at last, the music ended and, slowly and deliberately, Andreas put her away from him.

'You see what I mean?' he said. His

voice was husky and his eyes dark with desire.

Linda couldn't answer and they stared at each other wordlessly.

At that moment, innocent of any atmosphere, Espasia approached with Nickie. 'I put Nickie to bed now, kyria? — ' she asked.

Linda tore her eyes from Andreas. 'Oh — yes, Espasia. It's dreadfully late.'

Nickie, over-tired and excited, set up a loud wail of protest, and Linda thankfully excused herself, despite Espasia's protests.

When Nickie was asleep, she slipped out of her clothes and made for the shower where she let the water play coolingly over her heated skin. Then she towelled herself dry, slipped on her wrap and, going over to the window, stared out over the tree-tops to the bay.

She shivered despite the balmy warmth of the evening as she finally admitted to herself that she was falling overwhelmingly in love with Andreas Duncan — and that there were terrifying reserves of passion and sensuality in her she had never before suspected. If Andreas, who had treated her so correctly up till now, began to pursue her in the way that Gregori had, she would have no defence against him. Certainly she could no longer keep up her perilous masquerade. How easily he would break down her façade, would know, at once, that she wasn't a woman with marriage — and probably other affairs — behind her, but a girl almost totally inexperienced in the ways of men.

5

The following morning, things looked better. In the cool early air, Linda felt in command of herself again, almost scornful of her fevered emotions of the previous evening. What a ridiculous effect romantic music and a little too much wine can have, she thought austerely, as she took her shower. To say nothing of proximity! In future she would keep her distance, try not to be alone with Andreas, and things would revert to normal.

She put on a plain navy linen dress, put up her hair more severely than usual, and set off down the broad staircase. On arrival at the dining room she needed all the psychological support she could muster. Andreas was alone and the sight of him immediately turned her knees to water.

He raised an eyebrow at her as she

hesitated in the doorway. 'Ah, some company. I thought I should have to breakfast alone.'

Linda cleared her throat. 'Nickie is still sleeping, so I thought I would leave him,' she explained, wishing devoutly now that she had awakened him to accompany her.

'My cousins, too, apparently. They decided to go out dancing after you — left us. But we went early to our virtuous couches so, here we are, up with the lark!'

So he had decided to play it light. Thankfully, Linda slid into her seat and Andreas poured coffee for her. 'Where did they go?' she asked.

'Oh, to some big resort hotel up the coast. I honestly don't know why they come here. When they do, they live exactly the same life that they would in Athens.' He smiled with a trace of self-mockery. 'Maybe they are still too young to need to unwind.'

'Perhaps that's the way they unwind.'

'You should have gone with them. It

would have been — a diversion for you.' He glanced swiftly at her and away again. 'When you left us last night,' he continued, his voice less assured, 'I thought you intended to return. When you didn't, I wondered — whether anything had happened to upset you.'

She felt warm colour flood her cheeks. 'Oh, no. It was just that — Nickie took a little while to settle down. And I did have a slight headache.'

'The heat perhaps. It will be hot again today.' His eyes rested on her more lingeringly, taking in her dress that was fastened to the throat. 'You will need to unbutton a little later on.'

'Perhaps later,' she stumbled. 'I'm not at all warm yet.'

His eyes still appraised her. 'It's the early chill that brings the greatest warmth,' he murmured, and she was sure he was not only speaking of the weather. He excused himself from the table and strolled to the window. He looked out over the garden, and Linda

164

was tinglingly aware of the lean muscular power of his body.

'It's annoying that you can't use the pool,' he said. 'My other cousins are coming, after all. Maybe Helen will bring a swimsuit.'

'If she does, she will probably want to use it herself.'

'Helen's passion, at the moment, is horses. If I offer to take her riding she'll happily give up swimming.'

'When will they be coming?'

'In an hour, or so. So, if you'll excuse me, there is some work I must do while the house is still quiet.'

* * *

Linda let him go with relief. She had managed their first encounter after the previous night's shattering arousal of her emotions with fair composure. With a houseful of guests, the remainder of the day should be plain sailing.

She ate a second roll, spread with the delicious peach conserve. Maybe with some sustenance in it, her stomach wouldn't quake so treacherously in Andreas' presence. She drank a second cup of coffee, then went upstairs to see if Nickie was awake.

He had just awakened and was looking around for her. She took him down to the kitchen where they found Katina already seated at the breakfast-table.

'*Kaliméra*, Kyria Blair,' Eleni greeted her. 'You have eaten?'

'Yes, thank you, Eleni. I came down earlier.' Linda sat Nickie up to the table and buttered a roll for him. 'I believe more visitors are expected.'

'Yes, my cousins are coming,' Katina put in. 'They are very nice. They play with me.'

'That will be fun for you, darling.' Linda smiled at the little girl. 'How long will they stay?' she asked the housekeeper.

'For today, only. Lunch, maybe dinner. Is schooldays, not holiday yet.'

The housekeeper got on with her

work and Linda supervised Nickie's breakfast, then took both children outside on the terrace. It was already very warm and she pulled her chair into the shade offered by a young fig tree. She realised suddenly that she was in exactly the spot where Andreas had held her in his arms the previous night as their dance ended. A torrent of sweet, demoralising weakness flooded over her and she lay back in her chair, giving herself up to the sensuous languor of the sun's warmth, her fingers creeping up unconsciously to unfasten the top buttons of her dress.

It was eleven o'clock when the three younger cousins arrived. Again, Katina was the first to catch the sound of the car and she shot off through the archway to the front of the house, to appear a few moments later proudly escorting her cousins. Linda immediately felt more drawn to them than she had been towards Gregori and Ariadne. The girl, Helen, looked about fifteen.

She was already a beauty, but seemed quite unaware of it. The older boy, Alex, was thin, solemn, and bespectacled. The youngest of the three, Damon, was wiry and very dark, with a quick laughing mischievous face.

None of them spoke much English, but they were good-mannered and friendly, and made a great fuss of Katina, who blossomed under their attention. When Andreas appeared at the dining room door, they gave him their respectful attention.

'Eleni is going to set lunch out here soon, so clear your chairs away and make some room. Also, she might welcome a little help in the kitchen with all of you mob to feed!'

He had spoken in English, but he seemed to have got his point across. Damon began to move the loungers and Helen made promptly for the back of the house.

'Helen!' Andreas called after her. He spoke swiftly in Greek. The girl turned to Linda.

'Yes, please. You have my swimsuit,' she said.

'Is it all right?' Linda referred to Andreas. 'Won't she want to use it herself? It's got very warm.'

He raised a sardonic eyebrow at her, sprawling below him in some disarray, and Linda fought an impulse to rebutton her dress.

'As I thought, Helen prefers to come riding with me.' His eyes lingered on Linda's *décolletage*. 'We'd better find you some suncream before you expose yourself further. Your skin is very fair.'

Helen had continued towards the kitchen, the two youngest children followed her, and Linda was left with Andreas, and the two boys noisily rearranging the chairs.

★ ★ ★

Andreas sat down near her. 'You wouldn't prefer to ride?' he asked. 'The stables at Vatsianna have some good mounts.'

169

'No, thank you. I don't ride, and it's too hot, anyway. I'm simply longing for a dip. I'll take the children to the beach.'

'Then I insist you take Espasia with you, to keep an eye on them. Good heavens, girl, you haven't had any time off since you arrived!'

'It's only a little over a week,' Linda protested. 'And I feel guilty that I do so little for my salary.'

Andreas shrugged slightly. 'You'd be the despair of the unions!' He raised his voice. 'What about you boys? What do you want to do this afternoon?'

There was a lengthy and volatile discussion in Greek, before Alex and his brothers apparently decided, as interpreted by Andreas, to do the Greek equivalent of 'just mooch about'.

Helen returned and, assisted by Nickie and Katina, began to set the table with a variety of salads and cheese, home-baked bread, fruit and olives and jugs of wine. Eleni was supervising the finishing touches when

Gregori and Ariadne strolled out on to the terrace.

'*Kaliméra*. Good morning!' Gregori greeted the company brightly. He eyed the repast. 'Good heavens! Is that breakfast?'

'No, it's lunch,' Andreas said shortly. 'Do you two have to spend half the day in bed?'

'I have to relax some time — '

'From what?'

'From the strains of big business, cousin. Anyway, we didn't get in till two o'clock.' He pulled a chair close to Linda's and turned the full battery of his charm on her.

'How beautiful you look this morning, Linda. How could I miss so many hours of your company?'

'By oversleeping, perhaps,' Linda said crisply. She turned away from him and began helping Nickie with his lunch.

Gregori spread crumbly feta cheese thickly on a roll. 'So — what is everyone doing this afternoon?'

'Helen and I are going riding at

171

Vatsianna,' Andreas responded.

'But, Andreas, you know I hate riding,' Ariadne protested. The Greek girl looked very attractive, Linda was forced to admit, in a pale pink sundress that set off her golden tan.

'I said I was taking *Helen*,' Andreas pointed out equably.

Gregori nuzzled his face into Linda's averted shoulder. 'What are your plans?' he murmured.

'I'm going to take the children to the beach. Helen has kindly lent me a swimsuit.'

'I can't wait to see it! The beach for me, then.'

Both Andreas and Ariadne glared at him. Andreas got in first.

'I think you'd better accompany us to Vatsianna, Gregori. There are a number of business matters I need to discuss with you and, since you rarely seem to make yourself available in the office — '

'You've got to be joking! We can talk now — or at dinner.'

'I am not joking, and I have no

172

intention of inflicting business on the company at mealtimes. You will come to Vatsianna.'

There was an awkward pause before Gregori, obviously realising that dispute was impossible, shrugged with ill-grace.

'And I?' Ariadne enquired equally sullenly. 'I suppose I go to the beach with the children?'

It was not an arrangement that Linda looked forward to with much pleasure. Ariadne had scarcely exchanged a word with her since she had arrived and was unlikely to make an agreeable companion, but the prospect, on such a hot and sticky day, of swimming in those aquamarine waters was too glorious to be spoiled.

* * *

The high spirits of the younger members around the lunch table soon restored a pleasant atmosphere and, when they'd finished eating, they went their separate ways. Alex and Damon

173

were the first to disappear, then Helen fetched her bag from her brother's car, and, unzipping it, hauled out a pale-blue bikini.

To say the garment was brief was an understatement. It was microscopic, and Linda couldn't hide her dismay as she regarded the scraps of material. She hadn't expected that Helen would wear so revealing a swimsuit, but the fifteen-year-old was smaller than she was and not yet fully developed.

'Will it fit?' Helen was enquiring. 'I do not wear it since one year, when I am small.'

'Andreas, you wouldn't be so cruel!' Gregori was groaning in mock anguish. 'I must go to the beach!'

'Does Ariadne not have a swimsuit to lend?' Helen said. 'She is more fat.'

Her innocently poor English provoked a snigger from Gregori and a look of fury from Ariadne.

'I shall be wearing mine, stupid one!' she snapped.

'Thank you very much, Helen,' Linda

put in hastily. 'I'll try it on in my room. I'm sure it will be fine.'

She sped up to her room, undressed and wriggled into the bikini. It was *just* about adequate, but scarcely decent. However, she was determined not to miss out on her swim. She gave a last ineffectual tug at the garment and slipped her dress over it. She packed a towel, sunglasses and suncream in the straw bag and went back downstairs.

Ariadne was alone on the terrace. As Linda arrived, she slouched off into the house to reappear ten minutes later with an enormous beach-bag. Linda called the children and they went beneath the garden arch to the front of the house.

As they did so, the riding party emerged by the front door. Helen was flanked by her two male cousins and looked justifiably proud of her escort. Both Andreas and Gregori wore beautifully-cut riding breeches and white shirts open at the throats. Both looked strikingly handsome, though, in

Linda's opinion, Andreas' high-cheekboned, aquiline features gave him the edge. Helen herself wore jeans and was carrying an English hard-hat that must have been packed on the chance of getting a ride.

They got into Gregori's car, calling their goodbyes and whirled off down the drive in a flurry of dust, Ariadne's eyes following them wistfully. She heaved a sigh and trailed after Linda and the others, teetering slightly on her high-heeled sandals.

In a few minutes they emerged from the cover of the trees and Linda was momentarily blinded by the dazzle of the almost-turquoise sea and the silver sand.

Ariadne, still without a word to her companions, immediately flung herself down on to the beach, pulling a quantity of cushions and towels from her beach-bag. She took off her dress to reveal a white bikini almost as brief as Linda's and which, with her heavy gold necklet and bracelets, showed off her voluptuous beauty. Reclining on her cushions, she began lovingly rubbing cream into her skin.

Linda and Espasia changed the children into their swimming things. Espasia, who would not be lured within twenty feet of the sea, settled down a little distance from Ariadne, and Linda, a child on either hand, raced down the beach.

They flung themselves into the warm shallow water and romped and splashed together, the children entranced to see a grown-up behaving in such an uninhibited fashion. Then, after some twenty minutes, Espasia approached the water's edge and, eyeing the sea with some disapproval, announced that it was time for the children to come out. Linda handed them over, despite their noisy protests, then waded out into deeper water, dived into a wave, and struck out in a steady crawl.

After a few minutes, she rolled on to her back, lazily treading water. Above the clustered pine trees, she could see the long green roof of the villa, and the olive and lemon groves behind it. Adjoining their beach, separated from it by a rocky headland, was a much wider sandy bay. She paddled around idly for a while, relishing the tranquillity and the sensuous delight of sea and sun, until she became aware of an uncomfortable tingling in her face and shoulders, and turned back towards the land.

★ ★ ★

On the beach, she towelled herself dry, then released her hair from its confines to hang loose. Espasia and Katina exclaimed aloud at its beauty and even Ariadne opened her eyes sufficiently to give it grudging appraisal.

'It's only to dry it quicker,' Linda explained, somewhat embarrassed at the attention she was receiving. She rubbed cream into her tender skin, then relaxed on her towel, watching the children until, at four o'clock, Espasia decided that they had been in the hot sun long enough and should return to the house.

Linda sat up and began to put on her dress. She didn't enjoy the prospect of remaining on the beach with only the silent Ariadne for company but, to her surprise, Ariadne said, 'Will you not stay with me a little longer?'

Linda looked at her doubtfully. 'I really should look after Nickie, Miss Katrakis.'

Ariadne shrugged. 'The maid will take care of him.'

'Nickie isn't Espasia's responsibility.'

'Of course, I look after Nickie, Kyria Blair,' Espasia put in willingly.

'Well, if you're sure, Espasia.' Linda sank back on the beach again, but left her dress on over her bikini as her exposed skin was tender and reddening. After a moment, the expected interrogation commenced.

'You are young when you have the child, yes?'

'Not so very. I was twenty-two.'

'When your husband leave you?'

'We were divorced six months ago,' Linda said shortly, irritated at the personal line the conversation was taking.

'Why does your man divorce you? Did he take another woman?' Ariadne had turned her full attention on Linda. It was impossible to tell whether she realised how offensive her blunt questioning was.

Linda strove to keep cool. 'Actually *I* divorced him,' she said. 'And other women were a very small factor in the break-up. We were simply incompatible.'

Ariadne let out a ripple of laughter. 'Incompatible! That is a strange word to a Greek woman. Here is not that we should be compatible. In Greece we should be as our men ask. We fall in with their wishes.'

'So I believe,' Linda said drily. 'But things are a little different in England.'

There was a momentary pause before Ariadne started on a new tack.

'You like my cousin Andreas?'

'He has been very considerate to me.'

A faint sneer marred Ariadne's pretty face. 'I mean — you like him? He is handsome, no? I think, myself, my brother is more handsome. And he is more fun.'

'Miss Katrakis, I'm not looking for a — an escort — or anything else. To be frank with you, I've had more than enough of men for the time being.'

Ariadne subjected Linda to a prolonged stare. 'I think when you dance with Andreas last night, you like him very much.'

There was absolutely no response to that that Linda could honestly give. Deciding that attack was the best form of defence, she enquired sweetly, 'And you, Miss Katrakis — are you not engaged yet? I understood that Greek girls usually marry at quite an early age.'

She was rewarded by a flush of irritation on Ariadne's face. 'There is — an understanding. Surely you have seen how things are between Andreas and me?'

'Why, no. I had no idea.'

'Of course, Andreas must be very discreet. He is the heir to a great business. If his mother, my aunt Sophia, had been alive she would have arranged the match long since. But since she died, matters have dragged on. Andreas is much away and knows much freedom. Tell me, Kyria Blair, do you know Andreas in London? Do you know of his women there?'

'No. I told you last night. I only met Mr. Duncan a few days ago.'

'I think perhaps he has many women there for his pleasure. But they do not worry me. They are playthings. He would not marry one of them. Especially since Susan. Many times he warned Robert against a liaison with such a woman.'

Linda couldn't help noticing how Ariadne's English improved when she wished to pry or insult. Suddenly she could stand no more of the conversation. She stood up, slipping her feet into her sandals. 'If you'll excuse me, I think I'll go for a walk. I'd like to explore the next bay.'

Ariadne regarded her with unfathomable dark eyes. 'But, of course, Kyria Blair.' She rolled over gracefully to continue her sun-bathing.

6

Linda hastened towards the barrier of rocks that formed the boundary of the beach, her feelings in turmoil. It was difficult to judge just how rude Ariadne had intended to be. Greek women, she knew from Eleni and Espasia's conversation, were untiringly interested in personal relationships, especially of a romantic nature. All the same, even given Ariadne's limited command of English, Linda was sure the girl had meant to wound. But, even without Ariadne spelling it out, she knew what any advance from Andreas would mean. Given the sort of woman he believed her to be, he would use her as 'a plaything — for his pleasure'. And a plaything not deserving of any respect.

But the miniature paradise of rock-pools on the headland she scrambled over to reach the farther bay soon fascinated her, and she half-forgot her disturbing reflections as she examined the delicate rock-plants and tiny colourful creatures that inhabited them, before leaping down on to the sand of the second beach.

This beach was much more extensive than the one she had come from. Taking off her sandals, she began to walk along it, the sea rippling in little wavelets around her ankles as she drank in the breath-taking beauty of the scene. The deep blue of the sea merged with the sky, and the glossy green of the Aleppo pines made a dark and secret fringe along the silver sand.

She reached the far end of the beach to discover a sheer cliff-face she couldn't scale. She sat down on the beach, her back against the sun-warmed rocks and closed her eyes for a few moments. At least, it felt like a few moments. When she opened them again, the sun was much lower in the sky and it was decidedly cooler. She jumped to her feet and peered towards the other end of the beach. The low rocks over which she had scrambled were under water. That boundary, too, was now enclosed.

She quelled the slight panic that rose in her. At least she was in no danger. It was obvious from the line of wrack along the sand that, even at high tide, the sea never completely covered the beach. Furthermore, there was almost certainly a way up the cliffs somewhere.

She made her way to the top of the beach and slowly patrolled the foot of the cliff, looking for any sort of foothold, but she reached the other end without success. The cliff was not high, but it was sheer. The bay was quite inaccessible.

She stared at the point beyond which the Katrakis beach lay and considered the options open to her. She could wait for the tide to recede — but she didn't know when that would be. She could stow her dress and sandals somewhere and swim round to the other beach — but that would mean arriving at the

Villa Minerva wearing only a bikini — a solution she put aside as a very last resort. The only other possibility was to leave her shoes and try to make the swim holding her dress clear of the water.

Nothing daunted, she stepped out of her dress and rolled it up into a tight ball, then, stopping only to jam her sandals behind a convenient rock, she slipped into the sea. The water felt chill against her skin, but it was placid and she had no difficulty in swimming out to the point, her dress held aloft. It was just as she rounded the point that a solid chunk of water, swirling round the headland with unexpected force, hurled her back against the rocks, knocking the breath from her body and, what was worse, loosening her grip on the dress. Linda made a desperate grab as it sailed away and managed to catch the skirt. She tried, once again, to get round the headland but, with the mass of wet material impeding her, it was impossible to make headway against the current.

She paddled back to the larger bay almost weeping with frustration. She wrung some of the surplus moisture from her dress and spread it over the rocks. The warmth that was still left in the sun might dry it out a little and then she could try again. Having made her decision, she sat down at the foot of the cliff and endeavoured to summon up some calming thoughts.

In a very short time she was feeling extremely cold. The sun had almost set now and a cool breeze was coming in off the sea. She tried running on the spot, but the moment she stopped she began to shiver again.

It was at this minute that she heard the shout from somewhere above her. Hardly daring to believe her ears, she froze, listening, and it came again, this time distinctly calling her name. She raced down the beach to where she could be seen from the top of the cliff, waving her arms wildly.

'Here! Here!' she shouted to her unseen rescuer.

There was a moment's silence, then an uproar of sliding and crashing as stones and twigs rained down on the beach, followed, in a cloud of dust, by Andreas.

He picked himself up, glaring at Linda as she hurried eagerly towards him.

'Where the hell have you been?' he exploded.

She stopped in her tracks and, to her chagrin, her eyes welled with tears. 'I climbed over the rocks from the other beach to explore this bay,' she faltered. 'When I got back here the tide had come in.'

'Couldn't you have swum round? You can swim, can't you?'

'I was trying to take my dress with me and I dropped it and it got wet. So I was drying it out before I tried again.'

'Why on earth were you taking the dress? You have others, don't you? It could have been collected tomorrow.

No one would steal it, you know.'

She gazed at him miserably. She couldn't bring herself to tell him of her reluctance to turn up at the villa clad only in the bikini — from which he seemed to be doing his best to avert his eyes.

'Well, you're down here as well, now. That wasn't too clever, was it?' Her feeble attempt at defiance emerged as crass rudeness, but Andreas merely grunted. He strode to the headland separating the two beaches and studied it for a few moments. When he returned, he said, 'The tide's on the way out. We'll be able to climb over in half-an-hour.'

* * *

He looked at her standing, shivering forlornly, in front of him.

'My dear girl, you must be freezing,' he said, and his tone was gentler. 'Here, put this on.' He pulled off his sweater and slipped it over Linda's head and its

190

caressing warmth, straight from his body, was so headily sensuous that she shuddered anew.

Andreas put an arm around her shoulders and led her up the beach. 'Come back here beneath the cliff. You'll be out of the wind.'

'What time is it?' Linda asked.

He looked at his watch. 'Nearly seven.'

'Oh, Andreas. We'll be late for dinner. And I'm keeping you from your visitors. I'm sorry.'

'Don't be silly. You're safe, that's all that matters.' They found a sheltered hollow in the cliff and sat down on the sand. 'I'm sorry I yelled at you. I was nearly out of my mind with worry.'

She turned to look at him, then, seeing the expression in his eyes, looked away again quickly.

'How did you know I was missing?'

'Ariadne told us, finally. We got back from Vatsianna about five-thirty. Ariadne was at the villa, and Espasia and the children and, after a while, I

191

wondered where you were. Ariadne said you had gone for a walk, about four-thirty, she thought. By then it was nearly six-thirty, which seemed rather a long walk — especially as you had left your towel and bag behind. So, we set out to search for you. I took the coastline and Gregori went inland.'

Linda groaned. 'Oh, no, not Gregori, too.'

'He was more than willing,' Andreas said drily. He smiled at her. 'Are you still cold?'

'A little.'

He tightened his grip on her shoulders and drew her closer against him. Her loosened hair spilled over his arm and, below his sweater, her slim bare legs stretched out. Something like a shudder ran through Andreas' body.

She glanced up at him. 'Now you're cold.'

'No.' He grimaced wryly. 'That's not my problem.' Their eyes met and the air between them was electric with tension. Very gently, he stroked the mane of hair. 'Your hair is so beautiful. Why do you always pin it up?'

'It's — convenient,' Linda mumbled self-consciously. Suddenly, she was unbearably aware of his lean body against hers.

His hand dropped from her hair and slowly caressed her cheek and throat. She could scarcely breathe as she stared at him, her eyes enormous with panic. His own eyes were dark with passion as he lowered her to the sand, his body covering hers. A treacherous alchemy of desire seized Linda. She trembled uncontrollably and a moan broke from her.

As if it had been a signal, Andreas' mouth came down on to hers. The kiss started gently, soon to become sensually explorative, then hard and demanding.

Suddenly, he gave a groan and rolled away from her, swearing softly in Greek.

Linda's entire being cried out in loss. She sat up and buried her burning face in her arms that encircled her knees.

Andreas' harsh breathing quieted after a while. He raked a hand through his hair and, his voice almost under control, said, 'Get up. We can get back to the house now.'

★   ★   ★

Linda stumbled to her feet. She collected her dress and sandals from the rocks, pulled off Andreas' sweater and put on the wet clinging dress. She held out the sweater to him.

'Put it on,' he ordered tersely.

Thankfully she slipped the warm garment back over her dress, and, in silence, followed Andreas to the headland. The sea was still foaming over the lower rocks, but he leapt the eddies and climbed nimbly up, turning at the summit to reach back for Linda. His strong hand grasped her forearm and he half-dragged her from the beach to share his narrow platform. For a second she was held tightly against him, then he slithered down to the beach on the other side. He held his arms wide and Linda leapt into them once again to be held in a momentary embrace. The he released her, turned away and, still without a word, strode up the beach.

Cold, wet, and horribly embarrassed, Linda scurried after him along the track and up the drive to the villa. She ran up the stairs to her room, meeting no one, pulled off her wet garments, and took a shower as hot as she could bear it. Then she hastily dressed, tied back her damp hair with a ribbon, put on a trace of lipstick, and hurried downstairs.

Through the open door of the dining room, she could see the three young Katrakis cousins, and Ariadne, at their meal. Andreas and Gregori were together in the study drinking an *apéritif*.

As she hesitated in the hall, Gregori hurried out and embraced her warmly.

'Linda, thank goodness you're back! I was frantic!'

Linda was touched, despite herself. 'I'm sorry you had to go out searching for me. I hope I haven't spoilt your meal.'

Making the most of the situation, he still kept her tightly pressed against him. 'As though I could think of eating until I knew you were safe!'

Andreas had joined them, a glass of brandy in his hand, and was regarding them with a sardonic eye.

'Let her drink this, Gregori,' he said.

Reluctantly, Gregori half-released her, keeping an arm around her waist as she cautiously sipped the brandy.

'Where's Nickie?' she asked. 'Was he upset?'

'He and Katina are having supper in the kitchen. We tried to see that he wasn't alarmed,' Andreas reassured her. 'He's been told that you're back. Now, maybe we should go in to dinner. Alex must start back to Athens soon.'

The three of them went into the dining room where Linda was given a warm welcome by the young Katrakis cousins and by Eleni, who hastened to pile food on her plate. Ariadne's expression at finding Linda the centre of attention was more sullen than ever.

To her surprise, Linda found she had quite an appetite and she tucked into her meal, conversing mainly with Helen, who was seated next to her. The girl insisted that Linda should keep her bikini, assuring her that she had others, while Linda pressed her, in a low voice, to try to come back to the villa the following weekend. The thought of being alone with Andreas now, after their passionate encounter on the beach, filled her with desperate misgivings and the presence of the young Katrakis family would help to relieve the tension of the situation.

* * *

Soon it was time for them to leave and, with prolonged goodbyes, they were waved off from the front door. Immediately they had gone, Linda took Nickie

197

up to bed. He was unusually clinging as he had his bath and was tucked up in bed. Linda read him a story and, as she bent to kiss him, his arms twined tightly about her neck.

'I thought you were drown-ded, Lindy,' he whispered.

Linda hugged him. 'That was silly, darling. I just went for a long walk.'

'Mr. Duncan thought you were drown-ded,' he said stubbornly. 'He was very cross.'

'Cross?' Linda detached Nickie's arms so that she could see his face. 'With me?'

'No.' Nickie yawned hugely. 'With — with Radnee. He shouted at her.'

'Mr. Duncan shouted at Ariadne? What did he say, Nickie?'

Nickie concentrated hard, but the memory was slipping away from him and his eyes were glazing with sleep. 'He said — he said — it was her cruel tongue. But I looked at her tongue, Lindy, and it was just ordinny . . . ' His voice died away and his lashes drooped on to his cheeks.

Linda gently pulled the bedcovers over him. So, Andreas, more perceptive than she would have imagined, had realised that Ariadne had upset her on the beach.

Returning to her own room, she gazed into the mirror. A rosy glow, that wasn't all sunburn, flushed her cheeks and her eyes shone brilliantly.

It was only just after nine o'clock, but she couldn't face returning to the company, although she hadn't said goodbye to Gregori and Ariadne who were presumably leaving some time tonight.

She undressed and put on her nightdress and wrap, and was brushing her hair at the mirror when she heard a faint tap at the door.

Her heart lurched like a roller-coaster. 'Who is it?' she whispered.

For reply the door opened. Gregori stood outside in the dimly-lit hall, her beach-bag in his hand.

Linda didn't know whether the surge

of feeling that washed over her was relief or disappointment.

Taking advantage of her inaction, Gregori slid smoothly inside the room, nudging the door shut with his heel. He proffered the bag.

'Ariadne brought your bag up from the beach when you didn't come back. She also wanted to say goodbye — and so do I.'

Linda stood up, pulling the inadequate wrap around her. 'Thank you for returning it — and thank you for going out to search for me.' She put out a hand to take the bag. 'Goodbye, Gregori.'

Gregori tossed the bag on the dressing-table and took both her hands in his. His hot brown eyes gazed into hers.

'Oh, Linda — this is crazy! My going away when we have just met.'

Profoundly uncomfortable, Linda stammered, 'Well — you know where I am, now!'

'It means so much to me that you are

here. I'll come back as soon as I can get away.'

'I'll look forward to seeing you.' In a way, it was true. He would serve as another buffer between her and Andreas. But she knew she must be careful not to inject too much warmth into her voice. Gregori under the impression that he had something to hope for, would be very difficult to handle. As it was, it looked as though she had overdone it.

'Lovely Linda,' he murmured thickly. He pulled her into his arms. She allowed their lips to meet briefly, then endeavoured to free herself.

'You must leave now, Gregori. You really shouldn't be in my room, you know.'

'Because Andreas would be jealous — is that what you mean?'

'This has nothing to do with Andreas. Nickie is in bed just behind that open door and I don't think you should be here.' She smiled to take the edge off her words. 'Besides, my shoulders are sunburned and you're hurting me!'

★ ★ ★

For some reason this seemed to arouse him even further. His face flushed, he dragged the apricot silk off her shoulders and his eyes devoured her pink-tinged skin. Angered now, Linda redoubled her efforts to free herself. As she did so, she saw, behind Gregori's back, the door pushed open and Andreas standing in the doorway watching them.

As she stared at him, mesmerised with horror, he spoke coolly. 'Gregori, your sister is waiting to leave.'

'*Hristo*!' Gregori spun round with a furious oath. 'Have you been spying on us? That's sick! What's the matter with you? Afraid I'm poaching on your property?'

Andreas took a quick step forward and, for a terrible moment, Linda thought he meant to strike his cousin.

But he stopped short and, with a visible effort at control, said again, 'I'm telling you that Ariadne is waiting to leave.'

He stood aside to let Gregori pass him, his eyes cold with distaste. 'In any case, there's a child in the next room. I would have thought that even you would have drawn the line at that!'

He closed the door behind them and Linda was left staring miserably at its blank expanse.

'I just said that,' she protested wordlessly. 'Why couldn't he have eavesdropped a minute earlier and heard me say it? What kind of depraved creature does he think I am? First, my shameless reaction to him on the beach, and now, a mere two hours later, this with his cousin.'

She put out her lamp and huddled into bed, burying her burning face in the pillows. Wasn't the situation she had taken on difficult enough without this added complication? It wasn't her fault that she seemed to inflame them so. Nothing of the sort ever happened in

England, she thought, recalling David's lukewarm responses. Before she finally fell asleep, her pillow was soaked with tears of chagrin and self-pity.

She was awakened the following morning by the sound of Andreas' car on the drive. It was earlier than he usually left for Athens and she wondered if he had done it to avoid her presence at breakfast. Well, if he had, it suited her fine. She got up, washed and dressed herself and Nickie, and hurried downstairs. Her first action, as always, was to look through the mail to see if there was a letter from Julie and, as always, there was nothing. She went on to the kitchen, where Eleni was singing as she slapped a mound of bread-dough energetically about.

Linda sat Nickie at a corner of the table, fetched him some bread and honey and milk, and poured herself a cup of coffee.

'Mr. Duncan left early this morning,' she said.

'Yes, he says lots to do in Athens,'

Eleni responded. She brought hot fresh rolls and a dish of figs to the table. 'You like Mr. Gregori, *thespinis*? Very jolly man, yes?'

'Very jolly,' Linda agreed bleakly. She took a long drink of her coffee.

Eleni looked at her sharply. 'Do you not sleep well, *thespinis*?'

'Not very. My shoulders are rather painful from sunburn.'

'Such beautiful white skin, you should not put it in the sun! I have some cream I give you.'

When Nickie had finished his breakfast, Linda handed him over to Espasia and made her way to Andreas' office. There, she typed a pile of letters that were waiting on his desk and did some filing, before returning to help Espasia with the children until lunchtime. After lunch she had a brief rest on her bed, then swam in the pool. She had used the cream Eleni had given her and when, at six o'clock, she went up to shower and change for dinner, she was delighted to see it had done its work.

There was no trace of stinging left and her skin had turned to an even honey-gold. She couldn't resist wearing the Grecian-style dress which set her tan off beautifully. She made up her face with a little more care than usual before going downstairs.

★　★　★

Nickie and Katina had just started their supper and Linda sat sightlessly leafing through a book until, just after seven o'clock, she heard the slam of Andreas' car door and his footsteps in the hall. Only then did she realise how tautly every nerve in her had been strained for his arrival. He said something in Greek to Eleni, then he was in the doorway.

He was wearing a dark business suit and a white shirt, his tie pulled loose at the throat. His eyes were smudgy with weariness, and Linda thought how exhausting a long day in a Greek city must be, together with the awesome responsibility of running a huge business empire.

When he saw her in the sitting room, he looked uncharacteristically unsure of himself. He said, 'I told Eleni to wait dinner for a few minutes. I want to shower and change first.' He turned and ran up the stairs to return fifteen minutes later looking more relaxed.

He poured wine for them and gave Linda's appearance his full attention, his eyes ranging over her in frank admiration.

'Was this just for me?'

Linda looked at him, puzzled.

'The dress,' he gestured. 'The whole *ensemble*. I'm very flattered.'

Her cheeks flamed with colour. 'I couldn't resist showing off the tan,' she stumbled.

'Lovely,' he said quietly. 'As I'm sure you're aware.'

Eleni came in and started to serve dinner, and they took their places at the table.

'You will have found it quiet today,

after the company,' he remarked.

'Yes, it was rather.'

'Well, never mind. We have another visitor coming at the end of the week for a few days.'

'I don't know why you persist in thinking I require a lively time,' Linda protested. 'I love the peace and tranquillity here.'

Andreas shrugged sceptically and Linda recalled Nickie's unfortunate remarks on his mother's love of parties and dancing.

'This man is important to me,' he said. 'A vital deal is hanging in the balance. I simply don't have the time to devote to him in Athens, so I thought if he relaxed out here with us for a couple of days — '

Linda's heart gave a lurch. Andreas had allowed her into a corner of himself. He had revealed his anxiety, he had appealed to her for help, and in that 'with us' he had, if only for a moment, made them a partnership.

When she answered him, her whole

heart was in her eyes. 'I'll do all I can.'

He looked once more at the honey-coloured shoulders and the golden skin of her throat and neck. 'That's formidable enough!' he said, and his voice was husky.

Somehow the meal — and the rest of the evening — passed, not too painfully. Andreas seemed worried and spoke little, but there was a delicate bond between them, and no mention was made of the interlude with Gregori the previous night.

After dinner, he walked alone in the garden, while Linda curled up in a chair, under a lamp, with a book, until she excused herself and went up early to her room.

The days that followed reverted to the pattern of the previous week. Andreas spent long days in Athens. When he returned, there was the same bitter-sweet tension between them. Both were painfully aware of the other's every move and, when they passed in doorways or on the garden paths, a tormenting electricity seemed to leap the gap between them.

★ ★ ★

On the Thursday morning, Linda came down with Nickie to find Andreas still at the breakfast-table. It was the first time since the weekend that he had not already left for Athens and, instead of his usual business suit, he wore casual trousers and a sweatshirt.

He stood up as she entered. 'Good morning. I'm afraid you're going to have to put up with me this morning. I have to drive up to Kastri. Perhaps you would like to bring the children?'

Nickie immediately expressed unqualified enthusiasm, as did Katina, who entered at that moment, climbing affectionately on to her uncle's lap. They all finished their breakfasts, then went out to Andreas' car. He shut the children securely in the back and held the door open for Linda.

She sat back and looked out at the

same scenery she had passed on her drive with Gregori the previous Saturday morning, but this time, with further chance to enjoy it, as Andreas drove at a more reasonable speed, and related anecdotes about the people who lived in various houses along the route.

They parked near the spot where Gregori had done, but now the villagers, who had stood back regarding the visitors on that occasion, approached smiling. Andreas' attitude to them was markedly different from Gregori's rather feudal manner. He greeted them by name, shaking their hands with a remark, or a joke.

'I have to see the headman,' he told Linda. As he spoke, an old man leaning on a stick came from the open door of a nearby cottage. He approached Andreas and, after much hand-shaking, they returned together to the cottage. An old woman, dressed completely in black, came out to greet them. Andreas went inside with the old man and the woman brought out a jug of milk and a plate of little cakes, smiling as she put them down on a bench beside the high, outdoor baking oven.

Linda smiled her thanks and sat down on the bench, and the children, having each secured a cake, ran off to inspect a bad-tempered looking goat that was tethered to a fig tree. After a while, Andreas emerged with the headman and two younger men, and there was more talking and hand-shaking.

Turning to Linda, he said, 'Dimitri has given me the key to the church. Would you like to have a look at it while we're here?'

'Very much.'

She stood up, the children rather reluctantly left the goat and they all walked up a steep track behind the cottages to the little church.

'There was trouble over the village rents,' Andreas explained. 'Times are hard. But they have good olive-oil, so I'm taking some in lieu of cash.'

Linda thought that the Villa Minerva

could probably produce more than enough olive-oil for its own needs, but, no doubt, the villagers' pride would not allow their obligation to be written off. It was a tactful, face-saving act on Andreas' part.

He unlocked the heavy door of the tiny dazzlingly-whitewashed church with its squat dome, and pushed it open. Inside there was such a palpable aura of piety that even the children fell silent. The walls were darkened from the smoke of centuries of prayer-laden candles but, from the shadows, the gold of a score of icons gleamed. As they studied the austere Byzantine features and melancholy eyes of the saints that gazed out from the icons and the faded frescoes, Linda sensed, even more strongly, the intense distillation of feeling within the building.

As they came out into the blinding sunlight, Andreas said, 'The church is the centre of even the tiniest village in Greece. It's at the heart of everything they do.'

* * *

When they reached the village square, Dimitri was supervising the loading of jars of oil into the boot of Andreas' car.

There was much talk and laughter, and bold speculative looks at Linda and Nickie, which Andreas appeared to parry with good-humour. Then the children were settled into the back of the car and they drove off to noisy goodbyes.

'What were they saying?' Linda asked.

He grinned sheepishly. 'I don't think you would approve. Very male chauvinist. Put a little more respectably, they want to know what's the matter with your husband that you have only one child? But old Dimitri says you are not to be sad, God willing, you will have many more.'

'I hope so,' Linda said quietly. 'But what about you?' She risked matching his mood. 'You haven't even got one.'

'Oh, they've given up on me,' he said

lightly. 'Fertility prayers, pleas to the goddess Artemis — they've tried the lot!'

He concentrated on avoiding the excited children and dogs that surrounded the car. When they were clear of the town he said more seriously, 'It's not difficult to find a desirable woman, but the sort of women I meet in the west — independent, emancipated, used to much freedom — it would be impossible for me to marry.'

'Because of your position?'

'Oh, no.' He seemed surprised by her question. 'That's not important. I meant because there must be total trust and security.'

'But there can still be trust, even with a — a liberated woman. A finer trust, based on freedom and mutual respect. Not because the wife is — a possession.'

'That would be very hard for me to handle.' His voice was low and he concentrated on the straight road with unnecessary attention. 'I couldn't live with a woman who had much previous experience of men. Which does make finding a wife over sixteen years of age somewhat difficult nowadays!' He finished with an attempt at levity.

Linda tilted her chin. 'You're afraid she might bring scandal to your family?'

'No.' Again he seemed surprised by her response. 'It's simply a matter of temperament. I couldn't bear it. I wouldn't be able to control my jealousy.'

Linda was stunned by the intensity of his words. She said nothing for a few seconds. Then she ventured, 'Retrospective jealousy is very foolish.'

'*All* jealousy is foolish and degrading to the sufferer. But I know I wouldn't be able to help it.'

Linda was silent. It was obvious to her that Andreas was echoing, in kinder manner, Ariadne's jibes on the beach. She was sullied and secondhand. She swallowed hard at the lump in her throat.

Andreas was silent, too, for the rest of

the way. They were turning into the drive when he said, 'After lunch I must go into Athens to fetch my guest.'

Back at the villa they ate a light lunch. Andreas left for Athens immediately after it and Linda sat reading in the garden while the children rested. When they came downstairs, she took them to the beach for a while, then got them an early supper. The children were ready for bed, and she herself had showered and changed when Andreas returned at seven o'clock. She had been putting the finishing touches to the dining-table, arranging vases of sweet-scented blossom, when she heard the car. She slipped into the sitting room and, through the window, watched Andreas and his guest alight.

The man was of medium height and somewhat overweight; his dark hair, worn rather long, was beginning to recede. He wore a light blue suit of a silky material and the sun caught a flash of gold at his wrist. As Linda watched, he took off his sunglasses and looked towards the house.

A wave of faintness engulfed her and, if she had not clutched at a chairback, she would have fallen. She stayed rooted to the spot as the men approached the house, then she whirled in panic flight out of the room and across the hall to the staircase. She had reached the third stair as the front door opened and Andreas came in.

He looked mildly surprised to see her frozen, white-faced, on the staircase, but he ushered his guest into the hall.

'This is my secretary, Linda Blair,' he said to the man. 'Linda, let me introduce Bernardo Mancini.'

7

It seemed to Linda that an eternity passed while she stood there, clinging to the stair-rail. Andreas' bewildered expression increased as the other man advanced the few steps across the hall. Without a trace of recognition, he said, 'I'm delighted to meet you, Miss Blair.'

Linda managed to detach an icy hand from the bannister and offered it to the man. Her thoughts flew round like squirrels in a cage as she mouthed some greeting. Was it really possible that Bernardo didn't recognise her? It was true that apart from the wedding celebrations, five years ago, when he had pursued her tirelessly, he had only seen her on two brief occasions. And he would certainly have been acquainted with scores of other women in that time. But his own sister-in-law? And with Julie's maiden name?

She became aware that he was still in possession of her hand and was leering at her in the old familiar Mancini way, while she continued to stare at him like a zombie.

She managed to mumble an excuse, tore her hand away and fled upstairs, followed by Andreas' frown. In her bedroom, she closed the door and leant against it, as though to keep some intruder out. She was trembling violently and her heart thundered in her chest.

What on earth was she to do? Even if, by some miracle, Bernardo hadn't recognised her, the moment he saw Nickie, the game would be up. In all probability, he would take him from her there and then, and restore him to the Mancini clan.

She sat down on her bed, wringing her hands helplessly. It was no use hoping that Andreas would intervene on her behalf. This patriarchal family was the last place in the world to look for support. It was Susan and Katina all over again.

She heard Nickie now, outside the room, talking to Espasia, on his way to bed. She hurried to the door and snatched him inside. She was wondering whether to quiz him about Bernardo, when he said, 'Lindy, there's a man downstairs . . . ' He broke off and Linda could see his three-year-old mind striving to capture some early memory.

'Yes, darling?' she prompted.

'I thought . . . ' He broke off again, frowning.

Linda helped him into bed, tucking his favourite teddy under the covers beside him. 'He's a friend of Mr. Duncan's,' she said. 'A business friend, from Athens. Did you meet him?'

'I *saw* him.' Nickie put the puzzle from him, as of very minor interest. 'Lindy, can we go to the beach again tomorrow? Tomas knows where we can find a baby octopus!'

Linda did her best to display the expected enthusiasm. At least Nickie hadn't yet recognised Bernardo, but his half-remembrance suggested that uncle and nephew had been in contact fairly recently.

As she stood in front of her mirror, straightening her hair with trembling hands and thankful that her tan disguised her pallor, another aspect of the situation occurred to her. Andreas' business with Bernardo. Andreas had said — and she had sensed all week — that it was vital. Would the fact that he was sheltering an illegal child-snatcher under his roof blow the whole thing? Might Bernardo even suspect that he was implicated?

This fresh angle swamped her with further horror. Her hands trembled still more, and her legs felt like jelly. She could scarcely stand, let alone carry on any sort of conversation. But dinner would be waiting, she couldn't possibly dither up here all night. She screwed together the remains of her courage and walked downstairs.

★ ★ ★

She found Andreas and Bernardo standing in the open terrace doors, drinks in their hands.

Bernardo turned his attention on her as she entered and her heart stood still.

'Ah, Miss Blair. Now the evening is complete. Food, wine, a perfect Greek night and the company of a beautiful woman. What more could a man want?'

Andreas poured her a drink and Bernardo continued his heavy-handed compliments. Andreas was watching them expressionlessly, but he had asked her to entertain the man. Swallowing her fears and her distaste for Bernardo, Linda did her best to be hospitable.

During dinner, Bernardo quizzed her about her previous life in England, still giving no hint of recognition, and she began to hope against hope, that he really had forgotten her. She responded with a very selective biography that in no way connected her with Julie and, when the men's conversation turned to business matters, she wondered whether there was still a chance that she might get away with it.

From part of their conversation that filtered through to her, it became clear that Bernardo's involvement with Andreas was not the coincidence it appeared. She had already realised that, because of the recession in shipping, the Katrakis Company was relying more and more on its cruise line operation. The Mancini family had the monopoly of luxury hotels in the Eastern Mediterranean. They were the two obvious groups for a merger of interests.

Linda was grateful that the conversation largely excluded her. She found it quite impossible to marshal her thoughts as she picked, without appetite, at her meal. But when they had reached dessert, Bernardo suddenly turned to her.

'I believe you have a little son, Miss Blair?'

Linda's tongue seemed to cleave to the roof of her mouth and she stared at him wordlessly.

'I ran into him in the hall. A beautiful child, so very dark — quite unlike you. He might almost be Greek — or Italian.'

'His father is very dark,' Linda managed to formulate.

'Yes, I imagine he must be.' Bernardo raised his wineglass, his heavy gold bracelet gleaming at his wrist. 'What is his name, Ms Blair?'

His black eyes, glittering with malicious glee, mesmerised her through the candlelight. Panic swamped her and she was totally unable to speak.

'He's called Nickie,' Andreas said easily. 'A delightful little chap and great company for Katina.'

The moment passed and the conversation moved away from Linda again. He knows, she thought to herself dully. But why doesn't he say something? It couldn't be sympathy — not from Bernardo. Perhaps the deal was vital to him, too. Too vital to risk aborting it by exploding his bombshell.

The rest of the meal was a

nightmare. The talk became more general and Linda did her best to play her part. It seemed an eternity before they rose from the table and Andreas excused them to go to his study for discussion.

Linda was making eagerly for the door when Bernardo's voice stopped her.

'What I would most enjoy after that delightful meal would be a stroll in your beautiful garden. If Ms Blair would consent to accompany me?'

Andreas glanced at her. 'Linda?'

'Of course.' She shivered despite the warm air as she led the way into the garden between clusters of jasmine and oleanders, their blossom shining in the dark, their scent seeming now sickly and overpowering.

★　★　★

Glancing quickly at Bernardo, Linda noted, with a sinking heart, the cold implacable lines of his face. In the dining room doors, she saw Andreas silhouetted, watching them.

Bernardo looked her over, slowly and insultingly. He smiled his demonic smile. 'Well, my dear Linda,' he said. 'This *is* an interesting situation we find ourselves in.'

Linda's heart sank and yet, at the same time, she felt a sense of relief that the ridiculously unreal situation had been brought out into the open.

'You did recognise me,' she said dully.

He laughed unpleasantly. 'Surely you didn't think I hadn't? You're not a woman who is easily forgotten.'

'You gave no sign when you first saw me. How could you conceal your surprise so well?'

'I was prepared. Our host had told me all about you on the drive from Athens.'

Linda stared at Bernardo through the gathering dusk. 'How could he? He knows nothing about me.'

'He doesn't know the truth about

you, I realised that. He merely said that we should have peace at the villa for our discussions and that he had an excellent English typist who would transcibe our conclusions. I congratulated him on having an English girl living in at the villa. I may have been a little crude — you know how much my brothers and I appreciate English girls. He snapped my head off, but he mentioned that your name was Linda Blair and that you had a small son.'

'So, you see, my dear, one would have to be an idiot not to make the connection. The Linda Blair I knew certainly has no son. But her sister has — and he has disappeared.'

There was a lengthy silence. Hopeless as it was, Linda could think of no course but to appeal to Bernardo's better nature.

She said pleadingly, 'I know what we did was wrong. But Julie was afraid that Paolo was going to take Nickie away from her for good. He had men watching her, they even came to the shop where I worked, looking for her. They threatened me — they were very frightening.'

'That would be Mario and Tony. They are cousins. It was agreed at a family conference that they should search for Julie.'

'But Julie has legal custody of Nickie,' Linda insisted. 'I know Paolo has visiting rights and Julie agreed to them. She would even allow Nickie to stay with your family in Italy if she could be sure of getting him back.'

'But she does not feel she can trust us?' Bernardo queried smoothly. He glanced over Linda's shoulder. 'Your Mr. Duncan — who is so insistent that there is nothing between you — is watching us like a hawk. I suggest we move away a little.'

Before she could protest, he slid an arm around her waist and led her down a flight of shallow steps to a garden seat, half-hidden in a bower of roses.

Linda reluctantly sat down and Bernardo sat very close to her. 'Julie was right,' he said. 'We had no intention of returning Nickie once he was with us. No!' With an imperious gesture he stayed her protest. 'English law does not concern the Mancinis. Nickie is Paolo's son. His *son*. He is in no doubt that Italian law would sympathise with him. And if it did not — it is of little matter.'

* * *

'It is of little matter.' The words echoed hollowly in Linda's brain. The Mancinis, the Katrakis, the Duncans — wealthy and powerful — they made their own law, and the weak and defenceless were powerless before it.

'But Julie loves Nickie,' she whispered. 'He's all she has. Maybe she didn't behave like the perfect wife and mother — not in the Italian sense — and I don't know exactly what happened between her and Paolo. But she did love him and she was never unfaithful to him.'

230

'As Paolo was to her? My brother had other women. He admitted it frankly. Julie just could not come to terms with it.'

'That was a lot to ask of an English girl. They hadn't been married very long.'

'But Paolo gave her everything she could desire. Houses, clothes, jewellery, cars — '

'She wanted *him*! She loved him!'

'She wanted exclusive rights in him. That was naïve, surely?'

Linda sighed. 'It's no use. We could argue about it for ever. We would never agree. What do you intend to do about me?'

There was a moment's pause. Then Bernardo said, 'How much does Duncan know of this?'

'*Nothing.*' The last thing Linda wanted was for Andreas' vital deal to go down with her. 'And I've every reason to believe he would side with your family. Are you going to tell him?'

There was a second pause during which Bernardo's hand slid along the back of the bench to rest on Linda's bare shoulders.

'I haven't decided what to do,' he said consideringly. 'There is some truth in what you say. Paolo was not a perfect husband and, personally, I always liked Julie.'

Linda tried not to shudder as Bernardo's hand crept beneath the edge of her dress. Attempting a smile, she said, 'Oh, Bernardo, if you could just think about it for a little while! Paolo is completely unreasonable at the moment. When he has calmed down, I'm sure they can work out a civilised arrangement. At present they simply want to hurt each other.'

'I'm sure that we, at any rate, can come to a civilised arrangement. This is an awkward time for me. I don't want to upset the merger with Duncan, it's important to us. You say he would take our part against you. Seeing the way he looks at you, I am by no means so sure. Meanwhile — ' his second hand, warm and moist, came to rest on her knee

— 'meanwhile, the solution would seem to be to — sleep on it.'

This time, Linda couldn't control her shudder of revulsion. She sprang to her feet. 'Then we'd better be getting back,' she said desperately. 'We don't want to antagonise him.'

Bernardo stood up. His face, close to hers, was coarse with thwarted lust. 'Very well, my dear, we'll postpone our discussion for the time being.' He turned back towards the house, his expression a mask of polite courtesy.

They found Andreas still silhouetted in the dining room door. He looked swiftly from Bernardo to Linda but, before he could speak, Bernardo said, 'A beautiful garden, Duncan — and an enchanting guide!'

'Aren't they?' Andreas said enigmatically. He stood aside to allow them to precede him into the dining room. He suggested a game of billiards. Bernardo made it obvious that he would prefer Linda's company, but she excused herself and hurried to her room.

* * *

Once there, she collapsed on the bed.
The strain of the last few hours had
been devastating. What action did
Bernardo plan to take? she wondered
wretchedly. Something entirely in his
own interest, that was sure. She wasn't
simple-minded enough to think that she
had won him over to Julie's cause out of
a sense of justice.

But, for the moment, it looked as
though she was protected by the
importance of the business negotiations. If they fell through, or even once
it was safely settled, she had no doubt
that Bernardo would expose her to
Andreas and take possession of Nickie.

If it came to that point, was there
anything she could do? She had quite
a lot of money. She could lay low in a
modest London hotel until things
sorted themselves out. But first, she
would have to get to Athens. The few
words of Greek she had picked up
would make that part of it easier. When

no one was about, she could phone for a hire car to collect her.

She would have to let Julie know of this incredible development, and she wrote a brief note to her outlining her predicament and her intentions if a showdown seemed imminent.

That done, she climbed wearily into bed, but tension wouldn't let her sleep. If only she could be sure of what was to happen, and be prepared, then there was a chance that she could cope. But, as things were, she felt helpless. And beneath the apprehension was the knowledge that, if she had to leave, she would never again see Andreas, never hear his voice or feel his touch, and that prospect brought an ache to her heart that was almost more than she could bear.

She woke the next morning to the recollection that it was Katina's birthday. Her own worries, and her disturbed night, hadn't put her in the mood for celebrations, but she resolved to make the day as happy as possible for the little girl. Espasia had purchased her a birthday card in the village and Andreas had bought a handsome picture-book in Athens on her behalf.

She dressed herself and Nickie, and went downstairs with the card and present. There was no sign of Bernardo, but Andreas was having breakfast with Katina in the kitchen. Katina's eyes shone like stars as she showed Linda the gifts her uncle had given her. A beautiful doll, a silver bracelet, and — here Andreas grinned sheepishly as Linda caught his eye — a whole wardrobe of pretty, comfortable play-clothes. There were boxes of sweets and books and games that Andreas had delivered from the Katrakis relatives in Athens.

'And Uncle Andreas says, next week, when he has got rid of Mr. Mancini, we shall have a party!' the child announced happily.

'Shush!' Andreas cautioned, as Linda hugged Katina and presented her offerings, wishing that Mr. Mancini

236

could be so easily disposed of.

She sat down at the table. Andreas poured coffee for her and they listened to the chattering of the children. Why can't this go on forever, Linda thought. But at nine o'clock, he appeared at the doorway, pouchy and bleary-eyed, and obviously not in an amiable mood. He mumbled an ungracious greeting and Andreas bore him off to the dining room where Eleni served him breakfast.

Linda finished her own breakfast and helped to clear away, then took the children into the garden to play. They had a happy morning of games, followed by a trying-on of Katina's new clothes.

After lunch, while the children took a rest, she swam from the beach, then read stories to them until tea-time. Eleni had prepared all Katina's favourites for tea, and there was a sickly-sweet and highly-coloured cake that entranced the children. Katina was allowed to fetch Andreas to sample it, but he returned to his study after a few minutes.

There had been no sign of Bernardo since breakfast-time, but throughout the innocent pleasures of the day, Linda had felt her taut nerves straining towards the inevitable confrontation at dinner.

★ ★ ★

At seven o'clock, she put Nickie to bed. Then she bathed, changed into a simple blue cotton dress and applied a minimum of make-up, in an effort to make herself as unalluring as possible.

It was obvious as soon as she encountered Bernardo that her attempt at protective colouring was not successful. He was sprawled in a chair on the terrace, a pre-dinner drink in his hand. He made no move to rise at her entry, but his eyes ranged over her insolently.

'Ah, Ms Blair,' he greeted her. 'I was beginning to think that Duncan had spirited you away. Has he been keeping your nose to the grindstone?'

'On the contrary,' Linda said. 'I've had a day of complete leisure.'

'Did you swim?' Andreas had appeared in the terrace-doors behind her with sherry in his hand.

She took the drink from him. 'Thank you. Yes. I swam from the beach.'

'You have a beach?' Bernardo queried. 'A moonlight swim after dinner would be refreshing.'

'But not sensible,' Andreas said shortly. 'The access path is difficult, and there are dangerous currents.'

'A pity.' Bernardo continued to ogle Linda openly as they sipped their drinks. It was impossible to tell how the negotiations had gone, but clearly no revelations had so far been made about her.

However, as soon as they started dinner, Bernardo's expression changed to one of subtle malice.

'I haven't yet had the pleasure of meeting your son, Ms Blair,' he said. 'Little — Nickie, wasn't it? I love the company of children.'

'Female teenagers, maybe,' Linda thought sourly. Aloud she said, 'Nickie has been in bed for some time.'

'Do you have children yourself?' Andreas enquired of Bernardo.

'I have been blessed with three sons. Our children — particularly our sons — mean so much to us. I'm sure you'll agree, Duncan?'

Andreas seemed slightly puzzled at the significance with which Bernardo seemed to be investing the idle conversation. 'Certainly. I have no children of my own, but my family is very close.'

'I understand your brother's child lives with you?'

'Yes. Katina's mother is English — ' Andreas remembered Linda's presence and had the grace to look apologetic. 'I mean, she likes to — travel a lot. It was thought that Katina would be more settled with us.'

'Without doubt, that is best for her,' Bernardo agreed readily.

The meal continued in the same way. Andreas seemed to sense Linda's discomfort, and kept launching new and apparently harmless topics, only for Bernardo to take them over and introduce some sly comment that only she could understand. It was misery, but somehow she got through the evening, even staying for an hour after dinner with the men while they smoked and talked. Only one more day, she thought as she mounted the stairs to her room, feeling far more exhausted than the activity of the day warranted.

She undressed, washed, brushed her hair, and took a book to bed, intending to read for a while, but it was impossible to concentrate and, after a time, she put it aside and switched off her bedside lamp. She lay staring at the velvety black sky, set with brilliant stars, framed by her open window, and wondered if this might be her last night in this lovely place.

She must have lain awake for an hour before she sensed, rather than heard, someone outside her door. A moment later there was a faint tap at the door and Bernardo whispered her name. She lay rigid, scarcely daring to breathe. Had she locked the door? As if in answer, the handle was tried, then gently rattled. Her name was hissed again, more angrily, but still *sotto voce*. She lay trembling beneath the covers and, in another moment, heard him move away.

* * *

The next morning Linda came downstairs determined to keep out of Bernardo's way. She had an early breakfast in the kitchen with Eleni and Tomas and, on hearing that Tomas had to drive into Kastri, begged a lift for herself and the children.

They were all assembled at ten o'clock and Tomas drove Andreas' car along the now familiar route, entertaining her as best he could in his few words of English. When they arrived at the village square, Tomas made a brief visit to the general store, then set off to call on the village headman. Linda and the children sat outside the *kafenion* where she ordered fruit drinks for them all.

All too soon, Tomas was back at the car and they returned to the villa where Linda played with the children in the remotest corners of the garden, then helped to prepare lunch which she ate in the kitchen.

She was congratulating herself on getting safely through the day when, with the children resting on their beds, she took a book out to a poolside chair, to encounter Andreas and Bernardo in the pool. Andreas was swimming and Bernardo sat on the edge, a glass of wine in his hand. He spotted her before she had a chance to retreat.

'Ah, Ms Blair! Again you hide yourself away. Come and swim with us!'

Linda pictured Helen's skimpy bikini and shuddered. She sat down in the chair farthest from him, put on her sunglasses and opened her book. 'I have no swimsuit, Mr. Mancini.'

He shook a roguish finger at her. 'Not true. Yesterday you say that you swim at the beach.'

'I borrowed a swimsuit.' Linda's tone of flat finality implied that the swimsuit was no longer available.

Andreas pulled himself up on to the edge of the pool, shaking the water from his thick dark hair and Linda couldn't help comparing his flat stomach with Bernardo's flabby paunch.

But modesty was not among Bernardo's virtues and he continued to press Linda to join them until, sensing her irritation, Andreas said, 'If you don't want to swim yourself, Mancini, we might as well go back inside and iron out those concessions in Genoa.'

In answer, Bernardo slid into the water and completed a couple of lumbering circuits of the pool. Then he hauled himself heavily out, tied on a bathrobe, and led the way back to the house without another word.

Linda watched them go from behind her sunglasses. Then she tried to concentrate on her book until Nickie and Katina came down at three o'clock.

The children played in the pool, then Linda read to them until tea-time. Afterwards, as it was Espasia's day off, she helped with the preparations for dinner, then bathed the children and put them to bed.

There was nothing to do now but to prepare herself for dinner and, what she fervently hoped was her last encounter with Bernardo. She selected the Grecian-style white dress that she had worn on the evening of Gregori's 'party', but didn't risk the stimulus of flowers in her hair, and put on very little make-up.

Once again she delayed going downstairs as long as she possibly could. When she reached the dining room, she saw Andreas and Bernardo on the terrace and reluctantly went to join them.

Bernardo was seated, a drink, as

usual, in his hand. He ignored Linda's arrival, but Andreas, standing apart, smiled a greeting, although he, too, seemed withdrawn.

Soon they went into the dining room and it was the same throughout the entire meal. The two men hardly spoke, and Linda wondered whether their negotiations had broken down, or simply that, outside of business, they had nothing whatever in common. It was left to her to make what conversation she could to ease the atmosphere and she found herself chattering nervously.

At the earliest opportunity, she excused herself and escaped to her room where she read for a while before falling asleep.

★ ★ ★

After her two disturbed nights, she slept deeply and it was only gradually that the sound outside her door penetrated her unconscious. She lay for a moment, not even sure of where she was, until it came again — her name hissed, the furtive rattle of the door handle.

At once she sat upright trembling, her mouth dry. 'Oh, God, make him go away,' she prayed.

But there was to be no easy dismissal tonight.

'Linda.' The hoarse whisper was urgent. 'Open the door, or I go straight to Duncan and tell him everything. Open up! I have a message from Paolo. He wants to do a deal with Julie.'

Linda crept out of bed and put her lips to the door. 'Go away, please, Bernardo,' she whispered. 'We can talk about it in the morning.'

'No. We'll talk now. Paolo is going to the States for six months and he couldn't take Nickie, anyway.'

'We'll talk about it tomorrow,' Linda repeated.

'I don't think either of us will be here tomorrow when Duncan hears the truth about you.' Bernardo's voice, slurred with drink, rose alarmingly.

With the greatest misgiving, Linda unlocked the door and half-dragged him inside. '*Please* keep your voice down,' she begged.

She had the foresight to don her homely towelling robe, but it didn't seem to douse Bernardo's ardour. His eyes burning hotly, he stared at her as though she was naked. Then he swayed slightly and leant back against the door to keep his balance.

'Now, what's all this about Paolo?' Linda asked briskly. 'Is there really a change in his attitude?'

'Beautiful, beautiful . . . ' Bernardo was crooning, still goggling at her. 'Why didn't Paolo marry you? You make Julie look third-rate.'

'This isn't a beauty contest. In any case, I haven't the slightest interest in your brother.'

'No, he is like Julie. A juvenile, a lightweight. But we are mature people, eh, Linda?'

He lurched forward suddenly, grabbing at her, and the force of his impetus propelled them both backwards on to the bed.

Horrified at finding herself in the very last place she wanted to be, Linda struggled upright, still clutching her robe around her; but the contact had inflamed Bernardo. He wrenched the robe off her in an easy movement and pressed her down on to the bed beneath his own weight.

He seemed almost beside himself with passion, and was frighteningly strong. His arms around her pinioned her own to her sides and he arched her back painfully to meet his body. His mouth, smelling strongly of wine, sought hers and she twisted her head desperately from side-to-side in fear and revulsion.

'No, please, no!' she entreated over and over again, but his only reply was to groan her name through shudders of uncontrollable desire.

His hand twisted cruelly in her hair and she cried out in pain before his hot demanding mouth came down on hers.

His other hand clawed the thin satin straps from her shoulders. But Nickie had heard her cry and, at that moment, awoke with a wail of alarm.

The sound startled Bernardo. Obviously dismayed that there was someone in the inner room, he raised himself off Linda momentarily, glancing towards Nickie's door.

Seizing her chance, Linda kicked out strongly with her imprisoned legs, squirmed from beneath Bernardo and, without thinking what she was doing, fled from the room to crouch panting and trembling in the hall.

★　★　★

In the next moment, two things happened simultaneously. Andreas opened his bedroom door and stood looking down the corridor to the source of the disturbance, and Bernardo slunk out of Linda's room arranging his dressing-gown around him. He glared at the quaking Linda and she held her breath, waiting for the inevitable. But he only edged down the corridor towards Andreas, muttering something about looking for the bathroom, before darting into his own room.

Andreas slowly advanced towards Linda. He wore a dark dressing-gown and his fingers still marked the page of a book he had been reading. She thought he was quite expressionless but, as he drew nearer, she saw the cool distaste on his fine-boned austere face, and felt cheap and soiled in the silly little scrap of silk that now covered even less of her.

Her face crimson, she pulled at the shoulder straps, but the top of the garment was ripped down and she crossed her arms in front of her to conceal her exposed breasts.

Andreas spoke at last. 'You put me in rather a quandary, Linda. Do I knock him down — or congratulate him? My upstairs floor has never been so popular. Perhaps I should install a turnstile — or revolving doors.'

Linda stared at him, speechless with misery.

'What happened? I'm aware that Mancini was in your room last night. Did it get out of hand this time?'

She was stung to words. 'He wasn't in my room last night. He came to the door, but I didn't open it.'

'If it isn't a foolish question, what prompted you to unlock your door tonight? Anyone could see the sort of man he is.'

She racked her brains desperately for an explanation of her action, but there was none except the obvious one that Andreas had assumed. The unshed tears, brilliant behind her eyes, welled and threatened to spill over.

'I didn't want to make trouble,' she faltered. 'I mean, over your business talks. You told me to entertain him.'

She had never seen him so angry. His eyes blazed at her and she thought for a moment he would strike her.

'Good grief, is that really how you think I see you? As a — an entertainment girl? I'm not a procurer! I don't lay on hospitality of that sort for visiting executives.' His voice rose to a shout and Nickie now began to howl in earnest.

Andreas struggled to regain his composure. His voice was icy as he said, 'Hadn't you better go and comfort Nickie?' But his eyes, in the second before he turned away, seemed to Linda to contain as much unhappiness as she felt in her own.

8

That night was the most painful that Linda had lived through. During the long hours, her mind replayed, over and over again, the scenes with Bernardo and Andreas.

Nickie had soon been pacified. Linda had flung the ripped nightdress in the laundry basket as though it scorched her, washed her face and taken some aspirin, before lying down on the bed to start her long, wretched vigil.

There was no way she could make things right again with Andreas. There was no possible explanation she could give for having let Bernardo into her bedroom. Not even an inexperienced girl would have done such a thing, let alone the woman-of-the-world Andreas believed her to be, unless she was inviting just what had occurred.

The only thing that could explain her

behaviour would be for Bernardo to reveal the truth about her position — as he was only too likely to do after the rebuff and public humiliation he had suffered tonight. And that would mean she would lose Nickie, perhaps forever.

It was no contest. Even if she had to endure disgust and loathing from Andreas, she was not prepared to give up Nickie if she could possibly help it.

All night her mind churned endlessly but, at last, the morning came. She rose early, showered, and was dressing when she heard the car drive up to the front of the house. She hurried to the window in time to see Bernardo leaving the house with his suitcase. He got into the car beside Tomas, without a backward glance, and was driven away.

Linda ventured a slight sigh of relief. At least that hated presence was out of her life. Surely he couldn't have said anything to Andreas? If he had, she would have been called down for an accounting, and probably been made to hand over Nickie. But why hadn't he done so? Was it still important to him to keep in Andreas' good graces? Or was he sadistically saving up his bombshell until later?

She glanced at her watch. Nickie was getting restive and there was no alternative but to venture downstairs. As she washed and dressed him, she saw her own face in the mirror; a washed-out pallor beneath her tan and dark circles under her eyes.

She crept downstairs, wincing at every sound from Nickie who was making a particularly noisy descent, hopping from stair to stair and carolling loudly.

In the kitchen she found Eleni.

'Good morning, *kyria*,' she greeted Linda with a smile. 'I make fresh coffee. Tomas he breakfasts early to take Mr. Mancini back to Athens.'

'Don't bother to make fresh, Eleni. This will do fine.' Linda poured coffee for herself and milk for Nickie, buttering him a roll.

'He leave very early, that man,' Eleni

was going on. 'At half-past seven he come to the door. 'I want to leave *now*,' he say, and Tomas must stop his work and go.'

'I expect he's a very busy man,' Linda said listlessly. She paused. 'I thought Mr. Andreas would have taken him in to Athens.'

'Huh!' Eleni made an expressive gesture. 'I don't think Mr. Andreas like that man so much.'

'Where is Mr. Andreas, now?'

'He is in his office, and he say, when you are ready, will you please go.'

'Go to the office?'

'Yes, *kyria*. But first you eat. You are so pale. It is the hot sun.'

'I couldn't eat anything, Eleni. I'm not hungry — Oh, for heaven's sake, be quiet, Nickie!' Linda snapped at Nickie, who was banging out a tune with his spoon, and Eleni raised her eyes at the first sharp words she had heard from her.

★ ★ ★

She drank a second cup of cooling coffee and made her way to the office on trembling legs. She knocked timidly and on hearing his response, edged round the door.

Andreas was standing looking out of the window of his office. He turned as she came in, meeting her eyes for a second, before looking away. 'I'm afraid there's rather a lot to be done,' he said. 'Do you object to putting in a few hours this morning?'

'No, of course not.' So it was to be business as usual. A fraction of the tension drained from Linda. But how could she let the ugliness of their last meeting lie simmering between them?

'About last night — ' she began in a low voice.

'Last night is over,' he said too quickly. His mouth hardened. 'I'm pleased to be able to tell you that the deal with Mancini went through splendidly. I suppose I partly have you to thank for that.'

'I'm glad it went well.' Linda let the

second part of his sentence go unanswered. She sat down at a small table where several folders were laid out beside her typewriter and started to rummage through them blindly, very close to tears.

Andreas obviously needed her services and he was prepared to behave as though last night had never happened. If only she hadn't fallen in love with him it would have suited her purpose, too. Simply to get through the allocated time until she could safely return to England. But, loving him as she did, how could she live with him thinking so badly, so unjustly, about her? A sob escaped her and she bent her head lower over the desk.

'Linda?' Andreas' hand covered hers that was still groping among the papers. 'I said it's over. Now, please stop messing the papers about. Put them back into order and type them up. Three copies, please. I — I'm going to see if Tomas is back.'

He left the room quickly and Linda

scrubbed at her eyes with a handkerchief. Struggling hard to concentrate, she applied herself to the work, temporarily almost forgetting her unhappiness.

It was after twelve o'clock before she had finished and Andreas had not returned to the office. She stacked her work neatly, stretched stiffly, and went outside, blinking in the brilliant sunshine.

The midday sun beat mercilessly down on the terrace, and Eleni moved slowly as she set lunch in the shade of the large fig tree. Linda offered her help, but Eleni refused, saying that Linda had worked all morning. She leant back in a chair, turning her face up to the sun and, in a little while, Nickie and Katina discovered her there and leant against her knee, telling her about their games. Her absorption in her work, the melting sun, the children's happy chatter, all combined to relieve her tension and, when Andreas joined them for lunch, the occasion was almost relaxed.

Immediately he had finished his

meal, he disappeared inside the house, and Espasia took the two children off to rest. Linda helped Eleni to clear but, when she returned to the terrace, she found her tension had returned and redoubled. She couldn't read, she couldn't sit still. She felt as though she could do nothing but weep. Restlessness suddenly possessed her and she found herself, despite the intense heat, striding up the hill behind the house as though something pursued her.

* * *

All at once her headlong flight exhausted her and she sank down in the springy undergrowth. Far below, through the trees, she could see the long terracotta roof of the villa and, beyond it, the glittering silver ruler where sea met sky.

She lay back in the bracken and closed her eyes. The heady scent of lavender, lemon and verbena was all-pervading. There was no sound but the drone of bees, the endless chirrup

261

of cicadas, the distant tinkle of bells from a grazing goat. The heat was stupefying. She gave herself up to its sensuous invasion, and anxiety gave way to simple yearning and misery.

If only she was here honestly, without deception, she thought. Free to feel the sun, smell the scents, enjoy the flowers and birds and sea. Free to play with the children. Free to love Andreas, without this black cloud of fear and mistrust hanging over her. The long pent-up tears began to flow as the cloud seemed to become physically blacker, cutting out the sun completely.

It was only when she heard a tiny crackle of the brush, that she jerked upright to see Andreas standing over her. As he looked down at her, Linda was painfully aware of her tear-sodden face and dishevelled hair. His own face was expressionless. Neither spoke for a moment, then he said, 'Tears for Mancini? I'd no idea you would be so devastated after such a brief encounter. But perhaps it's sufficient for you?'

Linda groped in vain for a handkerchief, sobbing harshly. 'I'm not crying over him,' she managed to get out.

Andreas proffered a clean handkerchief. 'What then?'

Linda buried her face in the handkerchief, glad of a means to conceal it. She leant her head on her knees. 'I'm crying over what you saw last night. You misunderstood it. You misjudged me,' she stumbled.

He sat down on the hillside at her feet and bent his head towards her. 'What did you say?'

His physical presence overwhelmed her, but somehow she repeated the gist of her statement. It was met, as she had expected, by a look of irritation and disbelief.

'My dear girl, what other conclusion could I be expected to draw? But — I thought you understood this morning — I want to overlook it. I value your services highly. I've been very happy about your relationship with Katina. But don't attempt to lie to me. I'm not a fool and I'm not going to be treated as one!'

Indignation lent Linda boldness. She flung back her tousled hair and her eyes blazed at him. 'I'm not lying! I was running away from him. Surely even you could see that!'

'He was in your room. You must have led him on until the thing got out of hand.'

'No!' Linda stopped. There was no answer to his inference and she knew it. She shook her head helplessly.

Andreas put a hand on her arm.

'Look, can't we forget it?' he asked gently. 'Can't we go on as we were?'

'How can we?' She raised her face to his. 'I couldn't bear it.'

Their eyes met. For a long moment Andreas looked at her soft, quivering mouth, her tear-bright eyes and tumbled hair, the curves of her body to which her T-shirt clung. His hand moved slowly up her arm and his other hand slid around her shoulders.

'Oh, Linda darling,' he murmured

and pulled her into his arms. His lips touched her eyes, her hair, her throat, then his mouth claimed hers in a long and passionate kiss.

He lowered her on to the hillside, his mouth still on hers, his hands tenderly caressing her face. A great flood of happiness and relief surged over Linda. He believed her, he loved her. She put her arms around him, stroking his long, muscular back and the curling tendrils of his dark hair.

She heard his breathing grow harsh and felt his mouth more insistent on hers. His hand slid up beneath her T-shirt to fondle her breasts, and her whole body seemed to melt with desire.

There was to be no turning back this time. Andreas was near the point of no return and she was eager to receive his love. But there must be no more deception. When she gave herself to him there must be complete honesty.

She gently pushed him away from her.

'No,' she began breathlessly.

'*No?*' Andreas raised his head to look at her in disbelief.

'No, Andreas,' Linda rushed on. 'I want to tell you about Bernardo — '

'*Bernardo?* You were on first-name terms? I thought he was a pretty repulsive fellow, but there's no accounting for tastes. And Gregori — well, Gregori has his success with girls, but I would have thought he was a little immature for you. What about Tomas? Doesn't a simple son-of-the-soil turn you on? Anyone except me!'

'No, no!' she protested again, but he had pulled her back into his arms and her words were smothered as his mouth covered hers. All her long-subdued sensuality was aroused as their bodies clung together. All she wanted now — on any terms — was his love. Her breath grew quicker and her body quivered helplessly as the tide of desire engulfed her and she gave herself to him. There was a long moment of mingled ecstasy and pain, and a moan broke from her.

Andreas pulled away from her, his face a caricature of incredulity.

'No! Linda, why didn't you tell me?' he exclaimed.

Linda put out her hand to touch his face. 'I tried to tell you,' she murmured. She yearned to lie for a gentle aftermath in his arms but, backing away from her, the look of almost comic horror still on his face, he turned and stumbled away down the hill.

'Andreas!' she called, but her voice faltered as she remembered his expression. It was clear that he'd expected a free-and-easy experienced woman, eager for sexual adventure. Instead, he'd found she was completely inexperienced and untouched. Perhaps he thought her attempt to delay him had been an attempt to defend her chastity. In any case, given his feelings about the purity of women, even having been deceived into believing she was the mother of a child, she didn't think he would easily forgive himself. Or maybe he thought the whole set-up was a trick to trap him into marriage. Linda bit back a groan of misery.

For her to stay on at the villa was now unthinkable. She would finish packing and telephone for a car from Athens, if necessary spending the night there if there was no flight until morning. At least there would be no need for secrecy now, she could plan her departure openly.

She looked at her watch, surprised to see that it was still only five o'clock. She tidied her hair as best she could, shaking the little fronds of bracken from it, and straightened her clothes.

★ ★ ★

She set off down the hillside, through the villa garden, across the terrace, and in through the dining room doors. In her room she took off her clothes and showered, put on a fresh dress, and finished her packing, working steadily and unemotionally like an automaton. When she had finished she went down to the hall and telephoned a hire-car firm in Athens to send a car.

She had just replaced the receiver when Eleni entered the hall.

'Ah, Miss Linda, there you are! We have wondered, you do not come for tea. Do you wish tea now?'

'No, thank you, Eleni. Do you know where Nickie is?'

'I think he is in the lemon grove with Espasia, *kyria*. Do you know where Mr. Andreas is?'

'No, I don't.'

Eleni looked puzzled. 'He go out in the car at half-past-four. He drive very fast. He do not say he will be in for dinner.'

'Well, he usually is, isn't he?'

'*Now* he is.' The woman's arch smile made Linda feel slightly sick. She turned away.

'I'll go and fetch Nickie,' she said.

'Not bedtime yet.'

'I want him here.'

Eleni glanced at her in surprise, but Linda left the house and went out through the gardens, towards the lemon grove. Only when she heard the children's voices at play in the distance did she falter.

For the first time, she wondered at the effect her precipitate flight would have on other people. Not Nickie, so much. He would shed a few tears, but would soon be excited at the prospect of the flight and the reunion with his mother. But Eleni and Espasia must be hurt and bewildered at her sudden, unexplained departure. And, most of all, Katina, who had obviously grown to love her and Nickie.

She walked on more slowly. There was no alternative to leaving, but somehow she must reassure Katina that she cared for her.

She saw the children as soon as she entered the lemon grove. They were crouched on the earth, dusty and happy, engrossed in building a fortification with some stones that had fallen from the dry-stone wall.

Linda stood and watched them for a

moment, then she said, 'Come along, Nickie, we have to go.'

Nickie looked up, squinting in the sun. 'Is it bedtime, Lindy?'

To avoid a scene she answered, 'Yes, it's bedtime.'

Nickie brushed his dusty hands on his trousers and trotted off ahead of her obediently. As Linda had feared, Katina slipped a hand in hers and prepared to come, too.

She said, 'You don't have to come yet, Katina.'

Katina smiled up at her. 'I go with Nickie.'

'No.' Linda swallowed hard. She looked around desperately and saw Espasia making towards them.

She knelt down in front of the little girl and took both her hands in her own. 'The thing is, darling, Nickie isn't going to bed. We have to go. We have to leave the villa.'

Katina looked at her steadily. At last she said, 'You, too?'

'Yes, Katina.' Linda hugged the child

close. 'Now, be a good girl and work at your reading and — and someday I'll come back and see you again.'

Katina flung her arms around Linda's neck, holding on desperately. 'Oh, don't go away, Linda. Please don't go away. I'll be good.'

It was almost more than Linda could do to hold back her tears. 'You *are* a good girl,' she said. 'You're my darling, but I — we have to go.'

Katina began to weep noisily and Nickie, sensing the drama, returned and joined in.

Espasia hastened her steps and looked at Linda enquiringly across Katina's head.

Linda unwound Katina's clinging arms. 'Espasia, I have to leave the villa. Will you please keep Katina here?'

'Leave? For all time?' Espasia stared.

'Probably.'

To Linda's horror, Espasia's eyes now brimmed with tears and she had a vision of a scene from a Greek tragedy with all four of them howling in the lemon grove.

'Goodbye, Espasia.' She thrust Katina towards the nursery maid and, grabbing Nickie's hand, hurried him towards the house.

As they entered the hall, Eleni, hearing the uproar, came out to meet them.

'*Ah, mikros ena!*' she greeted Nickie sympathetically. 'He not want to go to bed.'

Nickie snatched his hand from Linda's grasp and ran to bury his face in Eleni's comfortable waist.

'I've got to get this all over at once,' Linda thought. 'I can't go through it again in a few minutes.'

She said, 'Nickie's upset because we're leaving, Eleni. I have to go home.'

Eleni looked bewildered and Linda thought she hadn't understood. Then she said, 'You don't come back?'

'No, I don't expect so.'

'But — but Mr. Andreas?'

'Mr. Andreas would want me to leave.'

Without another word, Eleni enfolded

Linda in her arms, Nickie squeezed between them.

For the first time since Andreas had embraced her on the hill, Linda began to weep. She clung to the older woman for a moment, then released herself, firmly prying Nickie away.

'Goodbye, Eleni. Thank you for being so kind to me. I've — I've been very happy here. Please say goodbye to Tomas for me.'

Eleni rubbed her eyes with the edge of her apron. 'When you go, *kyria*?'

'Very soon. A hire car is coming for us.'

Linda hauled Nickie up the stairs, leaving Eleni looking after them. In her room, she rubbed a washcloth over Nickie's grubby, tear-stained face, then left him sitting, snivelling, on the bed while she gathered their belongings together.

★   ★   ★

She looked, for the last time, round the delightful room that had become home

274

to her. Then she crossed to the window to take one last look at the sea and was amazed to see that, in a few moments, the sky had turned a dark ominous grey. 'Symbolic of my departure,' she thought bleakly, as a fat drop of rain landed on her hand. From out to sea came a low rumble of thunder. Linda withdrew her head and closed the windows and, as she did so, the hire car drew up at the front door.

She opened the door to see Tomas at the head of the stairs. He picked up her cases and carried them downstairs, while she followed with Nickie.

Tomas stowed her cases in the car and, returning to the hall, shook her hand gravely. Linda hugged Eleni briefly, then hurried through the rain that was now falling in a steady downpour to the car.

The car made a slow circle in the drive. Linda waved to Tomas and Eleni in the doorway, then turned to cuddle the crying Nickie. It was a sad contrast to the lovely day on which they had arrived. Now, the windscreen wipers could barely clear the volume of water.

They climbed the hill and, at the junction of the dirt road with the secondary road, almost collided with Gregori's sports car taking the corner recklessly fast. Linda sank back into the corner of the seat, but had time to note the blonde head near Gregori's shoulder. It hadn't taken him long to get over his infatuation, she reflected ruefully, and Andreas' recovery would, no doubt, be just as rapid.

The thought brought Linda near to tears herself, but she concentrated on comforting Nickie, stressing the airplane flight and the reunion with his mother and, before they had reached the outskirts of the city, he'd recovered some of his usual spirits.

She directed the driver to take them to the airport where she made enquiries about flights to London. The first was at noon the following day. She booked seats, then hastened back to the waiting car. She asked the driver to take her to a cheap hotel and, fifteen minutes later, they were deposited outside a shabby hotel above a garishly-lit bar near the city centre.

The receptionist was surly, but eventually summoned an elderly man to carry Linda's case up the two flights of stairs. The room she was ushered into was small, dark, stuffy and sparsely furnished. She was going to have to work hard to turn this into an adventure for the tired and tearful Nickie.

He was probably hungry, too. The rain was now a little less heavy and Linda returned to the reception desk to ask whether it was possible to get anything to eat. She was directed to a take-away café further down the street. Persuading Nickie to wait in the hotel, she tied a scarf over her hair and dashed through the rain to procure a couple of burgers and cans of coke. At the sight of this unconventional picnic, Nickie cheered up further.

★ ★ ★

It was a dreadful night. The bed was uncomfortable. The air was hot, sticky and far from fresh. The room was lit by intermittent flashes of neon from the sign over the bar, augmented by a distant electric storm. The din from the bar rose until the early hours when the revellers began to blunder noisily around the hotel staircase and passage-ways.

Linda rose very early, thankful that, at last, the night was over. She drew back the curtain to see a pale opal, rain-washed sky. She washed and bathed her tired eyes and, as soon as Nickie was awake, they went out and ate breakfast in a nearby restaurant. Then they walked in the streets and sat in the park until it was time to pick up their bags from the hotel and leave for the airport.

They checked in early for their flight. As they sat in the departure lounge, flicking through the pages of a maga-zine together, Linda wondered if anything had been achieved by her weeks of worry and heartache. What, if anything, did the total silence from Julie indicate? Had it all simply been a stay of execution?

Had she let Julie down? Perhaps someone with more experience of life could have managed things better. She sighed as she pictured Julie's dismay as she returned with Nickie, back at square one again.

'Mummy?' said Nickie, as though echoing her thoughts. Then on a rising note of joy, '*Mummy!*'

Linda looked up. Flying across the crowded hall, arms outstretched, was Julie.

Incredulously, Linda rose to her feet to be enfolded, with Nickie, in Julie's arms.

'Linda, darling! Thank goodness I got here in time. We might have gone on crossing in mid-air for ever!'

Linda was laughing and crying at the same time as she hugged her sister. 'But what on earth are you doing here?'

'I came to collect Nickie. Oh, Linda,

the most marvellous thing! Paolo came to see me. He has a new girl. An American. He's absolutely crazy about her, but he hasn't broken it to her yet that he has a child. He actually asked me if I would keep Nickie out of his way for a bit!'

'Julie, that's wonderful! But how did you get here?'

'All by myself, you mean?' Julie grinned. 'I'm not as helpless as you imagine, you know. I simply flew into Athens yesterday and asked the taxi driver to take me to the Duncan shipping office, and he did and that's when I met Greg.'

'*Greg?*'

'Gregori Katrakis.' Julie waved an airy hand and Linda noticed, for the first time, that Gregori was leaning against the far wall of the departure lounge, watching them with a tolerant smile. 'Linda, he's *gorgeous!*' Julie mouthed. 'Why didn't you tell me?'

'But you needn't have come,' Linda said faintly. 'You could have written, or phoned. In fact, I wish you had written, or sent some word. I would have brought Nickie back.'

'I got the impression from your letters that there were some things about the job that you liked — quite a lot. I thought it might be a good thing if you stayed here for a bit.'

'But what about your job at the health farm?'

'Oh, I gave in my notice. Now, don't look at me like that, Linda. It was really boring and life's too short to waste it doing boring things. All the guests were women, apart from a few fat old men. Anyway — ' she hugged Nickie to her tightly — 'I missed Nickie dreadfully!'

Linda smiled. 'What will you do now? Get another job?'

'I suppose so. But, actually, Greg has suggested I stay here for a short holiday first. Won't it be heavenly to be all together at the villa?'

The euphoria of the past few minutes left Linda abruptly. She drew away from Julie and her eyes clouded with pain.

'I've left the villa. Haven't you wondered what I'm doing here? I've left the villa and I'm not going back. We can travel to England together.'

'But why did you leave, Linda? I spent last night there and I could tell something had happened. The situation was absolutely fraught, but nobody would tell me a thing.'

'Have you seen Andreas?'

Julie's eyes grew rounder. 'Oh, yes, I saw him! I was terrified of him. He seemed furious. He yelled at me for putting you in this position. Had he just found out that Nickie wasn't your child?'

'You might say that!' Linda gave a bitter laugh only, to her horror, to have it turn to near-hysterical sobs. 'You could say he found out the hard way!'

'Linda, darling, tell me.' Julie was horrified at this display in her cool, self-controlled sister. She beckoned imperiously to Gregori and he came over and took charge of Nickie. Julie drew Linda to a quiet corner. 'Tell me,' she said again.

★ ★ ★

Somehow their usual position was reversed as Linda, struggling against her sobs, told Julie about Bernardo's arrival and his persecution of her, finishing with the scene on the hillside with Andreas.

When she had finished, Julie asked hesitantly, 'And it was the first time?'

'Yes. Unbelievable, isn't it — at my age? No wonder he was amazed.'

'Linda, how can you ever forgive me? To have been made to suffer by that swine Bernardo. And there was no need for it. If only I'd bothered to write, you would have known he was no longer a threat to us. But you must come back to the villa. It's only fair to Andreas. He's obviously appalled by what happened, and I think he's in love with you.'

'What?'

'I know I'm stupid in a lot of ways,' Julie said complacently, 'but this is something I do know about. And, what's more, Gregori thinks so, too. He says he's never known Andreas like this before.'

'I'm not going back.' Linda dried her eyes and her chin took on the stubborn tilt that Julie knew well. 'Don't you see? He's quite capable of asking me to marry him because he — he besmirched my honour.'

Her words were interrupted by the first call for her flight and she turned towards the door.

Julie caught at her sleeve. 'Take a chance, Linda! You took one once. Is that your allowance? One gamble per lifetime?'

Linda ignored her words. 'Are you coming, Julie? Shall I leave Nickie with you?'

'Just come back to talk things over. Just for a day.'

Linda's mouth set in a hard line.

'There's nothing to discuss and I certainly don't want to see Andreas again. Goodbye, Julie, if you're not coming.' She bent to kiss Nickie who began to howl lustily.

Julie kept her hold on Linda's sleeve and called to Gregori. 'Gregori, talk to her! Make her stay!'

Gregori strode up masterfully and began to reason with Linda against the background of Nickie's wails augmented by snivels from Julie. There was a second call for Linda's flight over the loudspeaker. She made an effort to pull away, when, with an impatient oath, Gregori plucked the boarding pass and passport from her hand, wheeled round and marched towards the outer door.

Linda's mouth fell open in disbelief and it was a second before she came to her senses. She tore after him. 'Gregori, give me back my passport!' People parted to make way for her and she caught up with him, lunging at his arm. 'Give them to me! This has nothing to do with you!'

'Nothing to do with me! Do you think I'm going to put up with Andreas in this filthy mood indefinitely?' He brushed her aside and strode on to the door.

There was a uniformed policeman standing beside it and, in desperation, Linda approached him. 'Please, help me,' she said in English. 'This man has taken my ticket.'

The policeman looked at Gregori who grinned, indicating Linda, Julie, and Nickie with a burst of rueful Greek. The man smiled sympathetically, sketched a salute and pulled the door open for him.

Spitting with rage, Linda pounded after Gregori to Andreas' car which was parked outside in the 'No Parking' area. Here he stopped, pulled open the back door and shoved Linda in. Julie and Nickie scrambled in after her and Gregori swung himself into the driver's seat with an air of self-congratulation.

Julie gazed at him, wide-eyed in admiration, while Linda fumed in helpless anger. 'This is absolutely intolerable! It's totally against my will!' she raged.

'I will be sure to tell Andreas that,' Gregori promised. He spun the wheel and they swept out of the car-park.

* * *

Little was said on the drive to the villa. Julie stole timid sidelong glances at her sister. Linda glared out of the window. Only Nickie seemed to be quietly happy at their return. When they arrived, Gregori pulled up in front of the house with a fierce crunch of gravel. He opened the door and gestured to Julie and Nickie to get out.

As he looked at Linda, sitting grim-faced in the corner, much of his self-assurance seemed to desert him. 'I'll fetch Andreas,' he mumbled and made off swiftly into the house taking Julie and Nickie along with him.

When he'd gone, Linda leant back in her seat and closed her eyes.

She felt beyond caring what might happen next. She had thought she couldn't bear to see Andreas again but, now that she was forced to, she must somehow anaesthetise her feelings and get through it as best she could, until she could get away from this place. A tear crept from beneath her lids. Then she heard a footstep on the gravel and opened her eyes.

Andreas was leaning down looking into the car, one arm on its roof. He looked ravaged and exhausted.

He said hesitantly, 'Won't you come into the house?'

'No. It's not my idea that I'm here at all.'

'I know.' He attempted the ghost of a smile. 'Gregori told me he kidnapped you.' He paused for a moment, then slid into the car beside her. 'If you won't get out, I shall have to get in.'

She didn't want him so close to her — and yet she wanted it more than anything in the world.

'You don't have to — '

'But I must talk to you. I don't expect you to forgive me for what I did. But you have to know that I shall certainly never forgive myself. That I should be responsible for such a thing with you — the person who had come to mean more to me than anything in the world.'

'It wasn't your fault. How, on earth, were you to know?'

He ignored her words. 'When I left you on the hillside, I just drove mindlessly. I had to collect my thoughts. Finally, I turned back to the villa. I wanted to ask you to marry me. I had wanted to even before . . . ' He turned away and stared through the front of the car.

'When I got back, you were gone,' he continued after a moment. 'But Gregori was there, plus an incoherent young woman with an incredible story which — when I managed to piece it together — made sense of the incomprehensible.'

'I thought at first she was Mancini's

wife. Bernardo Mancini, I mean. But apparently it was a younger brother. She didn't know of Mancini's visit here, but gradually, through the long hours of the night, I realised that Mancini had some sort of hold over you. I remembered how he had seemed to taunt you in conversation.'

'When he came to my room, he threatened to tell you everything if I didn't let him in,' Linda murmured.

He turned back to her fiercely. 'Why on earth didn't *you* tell me? I would have protected you. He wouldn't have taken Nickie from my house.'

'But Andreas — ' her voice stumbled over the name she had thought never to say again — 'how could I believe you would take my part? After Susan and Katina, how could I think that?'

He stared at her. 'What do you mean?'

'I mean that you keep Katina away from Susan. You won't let her see her own child.'

There was a long pause. Then he

heaved a painful sigh. 'I've begged Susan to visit Katina,' he said in a low voice.

'What? But you said — '

'Every birthday, every Christmas. I plead with her to come. What do you think I am? But always she's too busy. She'll come as soon as the skiing is over, or the Paris shows, or the trip with a new boyfriend. So — I am the cruel uncle who keeps her away. Better for Katina than a mother who can't find time to visit her, wouldn't you say?'

Linda was silent. Then she said, 'I wish you'd told me.'

His head went up. 'We have our pride.'

'I believed you had all misjudged her. That she was just a fun-loving English girl.'

'She's that all right,' Andreas said bitterly.

'And that you thought I was the same, only much worse,' she went on. 'When Nickie said his mother liked to go out dancing, he meant Julie — '

'There's nothing the matter with dancing, and having fun. If I seemed to disapprove — well, I suppose I was jealous of Gregori. I hadn't the time, just then, to dance attendance on you. I was afraid he might lure you away.'

'Oh, Andreas, how could you think that?'

She had turned to him impulsively, her hand resting on his arm.

* * *

He took both her hands in his and his eyes pleaded with her. 'Linda, darling, do you think there's a chance we could put all this behind us, and start again from the beginning?'

'But isn't there an understanding between you and Ariadne?'

'An understanding?' He looked puzzled.

'An unofficial engagement?'

Andreas laughed. 'Heaven forbid! Did she put that idea in your head? It's just a game she plays.'

'Gregori implied it, too.'

'Well, it's not difficult to guess his motive. No, Linda, I was very fond of Ariadne when she was a little girl. I suppose I still am, tiresome as she can be. But I have never in my life come near to wanting to marry anyone until now.'

Linda was silent for a long time. The gamble was bold and frightening and wonderful.

'Are you sure you really want it?' She smiled shakily. 'You don't have some idea of — of making an honest woman of me?'

'Linda, I love you. I want you with all my heart and soul. I wanted to marry you, whatever you were. Even if you had been ten times worse than my worst imaginings. Because I couldn't help myself. I couldn't live without you.'

His lips came down on hers very gently, but soon, urged on by her warmth, his arms crushed her tighter, his mouth grew more fiercely insistent. With an obvious effort, he released her apologetically, but Linda drew him back into her arms. 'I'm not made of glass,' she said huskily. 'I'm a woman, and I love you.'

Lost to the world they gave rein to their feelings, as mouths, hands and eyes expressed their passion. Time stood still until, unexpectedly, Linda gave a little gurgle of laughter. Andreas looked up and followed the direction of her eyes.

Beneath the garden arch, Gregori and Julie had appeared, entwined together. Julie gazed up at Gregori with wide, adoring eyes.

'Oh, Julie, here we go again,' Linda said between a laugh and a sigh. 'Here we go again!'

THE END

We do hope that you have enjoyed reading this large print book.

Did you know that all of our titles are available for purchase?

We publish a wide range of high quality large print books including:
Romances, Mysteries, Classics
General Fiction
Non Fiction and Westerns

Special interest titles available in large print are:
The Little Oxford Dictionary
Music Book, Song Book
Hymn Book, Service Book

Also available from us courtesy of Oxford University Press:
Young Readers' Dictionary
(large print edition)
Young Readers' Thesaurus
(large print edition)

For further information or a free brochure, please contact us at:
Ulverscroft Large Print Books Ltd.,
The Green, Bradgate Road, Anstey,
Leicester, LE7 7FU, England.
Tel: (00 44) 0116 236 4325
Fax: (00 44) 0116 234 0205

RACHEL'S COMING HOME

Gillian Villiers

When her parents run into difficulties running their boarding kennels, Rachel Collington decides to resign from her job and return home to help out. The first customer she encounters is arrogant Philip Milligan, who is nowhere near as friendly as his two collies. Gradually though, he begins to thaw — but just as Rachel is wondering if she has misjudged him, it seems that someone is intent on sabotaging the Kennels' reputation.

HEALING LOVE

Cara Cooper

Dr James Frayne's personal life is in meltdown and it is beginning to affect his work. Becky, his Practice Manager, is deeply concerned and wants to help. But Dr James cannot afford to let her in on his secret — if she discovers what's troubling him, it could lose him his job. When his cold efficiency and her powers of deduction collide, sparks fly and emotions are stirred — changing both their lives forever . . .

ANGEL HARVEST

Glenis Wilson

Jennifer Dunbar's dream of becoming a successful lady jockey seems to be over when she has to quit to look after Ellie, her three-year-old niece. Ellie's mother, Rosamund, was killed during a thunderstorm. Mystery surrounds her death — and the identity of Ellie's father. Jennifer is determined to find him. But her search impacts upon other people, threatening to destroy not only their lives, but also her own. Then Jennifer discovers — too late — some secrets should remain secret . . .